THE TURN OF THE SCREW

by Henry James

OTHER BOOKS BY JOSEPH COWLEY

NOVELS

The Chrysanthemum Garden
Home by Seven
The House on Huntington Hill
Dust Be My Destiny
Landscape with Figures

STORIES

The Night Billy Was Born and Other Love Stories
Do You Like It and Other Stories

PLAYS

The Stargazers
A Jury of His Peers
Twin Bill (Women I Have Known and I Love You, I Love You)

NON-FICTION

John Adams (1737-1826): Architect of Freedom
The Executive Strategist: An Armchair Guide to Scientific
Decision-Making (with Robert Weisselberg)

ANTHOLOGY

The Best of Joseph Cowley

CLASSICS CONDENSED BY COWLEY

Crime and Punishment by Dostoevsky
The Brothers Karamazov by Dostoevsky
The Aspern Papers by Henry James
The Golden Bowl by Henry James
The Kreutzer Sonata by Tolstoy
Alice's Adventures in Wonderland by Carroll
The Portrait of a Lady by Henry James
The Scarlet Letter by Nathaniel Hawthorne

THE TURN OF THE SCREW

by Henry James

Adapted by

JOSEPH COWLEY

THE TURN OF THE SCREW BY HENRY JAMES

This book meets the requirements for ESL students reading at level 4 of the ladder word series.

iUniverse books may be ordered through booksellers or by contacting:

iUniverse
1663 Liberty Drive
Bloomington, IN 47403
www.iuniverse.com
1-800-Authors (1-800-288-4677)

Because of the dynamic nature of the Internet, any web addresses or links contained in this book may have changed since publication and may no longer be valid. The views expressed in this work are solely those of the author and do not necessarily reflect the views of the publisher, and the publisher hereby disclaims any responsibility for them.

Any people depicted in stock imagery provided by Thinkstock are models, and such images are being used for illustrative purposes only. Certain stock imagery © Thinkstock.

ISBN: 978-1-4917-8375-7 (sc)
ISBN: 978-1-4917-8374-0 (e)

Library of Congress Control Number: 2015919246

Print information available on the last page.

iUniverse rev. date: 12/08/2015

For Bernice

CONTENTS

OPENING

THE STORY HELD us breathless, except for the remark that it was as gruesome as a strange tale should be. I remember no other comment till somebody said it was the only case he knew in which such a visitation had fallen on a child.

The case was that of an apparition in just such an old house as this in which we had gathered—a sight dreadful to a small boy sleeping in the room with his mother, waking her in terror that she might see the sight.

I can see Douglas standing there before the fire, his hands in his pockets, staring down at us.

"Nobody but me, till now, has ever heard it. It's quite too horrible."

This, naturally, gave the tale the utmost price, and our friend, with quiet art, prepared his triumph by saying, "It's beyond everything. Nothing I know touches it."

"For sheer terror?" I remember asking.

He said it was not as simple as that, and that he was at a loss what to call it—for ugliness and horror and pain.

"Well then," I said, "just sit right down and begin."

He turned round to the fire, gave a kick to a log, watched it an instant, and then, as he faced us again, said, "I can't begin. I shall have to send to town."

There was a groan at this, and much reproach, after which, in his preoccupied way, he explained.

"The story's written. It's in a locked drawer—it has been there for years. I could write to my man and he could send it down."

It was to me he appeared to propose this. The others resented his putting it off, but it was just his sense of right and wrong that charmed me. I suggested he write by the first post and to agree with us for an early hearing; then I asked him if the experience had been his own.

"Thank God, no!" he declared.

"Then your story—?"

"Is in old, faded ink, in the most beautiful hand." He hung fire again. "A woman's. She has been dead these twenty years. She sent me the pages before she died."

They were all listening now, and of course there was somebody to draw the meaning of this.

"She was a charming person, but she was ten years older than I. She was my sister's governess," he said. "She was the most agreeable woman I've ever known in her position. It was long ago, and this episode was long before then. I was at Trinity, and I found her at home on my coming down the second summer.

"I was much there that year—it was a beautiful one; and we had, in her off-hours, some strolls and talks in the garden—talks in which she struck me as awfully clever and nice. Oh yes; don't grin: I liked her very much and am glad to this day to think she liked me, too. If she hadn't she wouldn't have told me the story. She never told anyone. It wasn't simply that she said so, but that I was sure she hadn't. You'll easily judge why when you hear."

"Because the thing had been such a scare?"

He continued to fix me.

"You'll easily judge," he repeated: "YOU will."

I fixed him, too.

"I see. She was in love."

He laughed for the first time.

"You ARE sharp. Yes, she was in love. That is, she had been. That came out—she couldn't tell her story without its coming out. I saw it, and she saw I saw it; but neither of us spoke of it. I remember the time and the place—the corner of the lawn, the shade of the great beeches and the long, hot summer afternoon. It wasn't a scene for a shudder; but oh—!"

He quitted the fire and dropped back into his chair.

"You'll receive the package Thursday morning?" I asked.

"Probably not till the second post."

"Well then; after dinner—"

"You'll all meet me here?"

He looked us round again.

Mrs. Griffin expressed the need for a little more light.

"Who was it she was in love with?"

"The story will tell," I took upon myself to reply.

"Oh, I can't wait for the story!"

"The story WON'T tell," said Douglas; "not in any ordinary way."

"More's the pity then. That's the only way I ever understand."

"Won't YOU tell, Douglas?" somebody else asked.

He sprang to his feet again.

"Yes—tomorrow. Now I must go to bed. Good night."

Quickly catching up a candle, he left us slightly at a loss. From our end of the great brown hall we heard his step on the stair; whereupon Mrs. Griffin spoke.

"Well, if I don't know who she was in love with, I know who HE was."

"She was ten years older," said her husband.

"*Raison de plus*—at that age! But it's rather nice, his not telling."

"Forty years!" Griffin put in.

"With this story he'll tell all at last."

"This telling all," I returned, "will make a great occasion of Thursday night;" and everyone so agreed.

I knew the next day that a letter had gone off to his London apartments. The manuscript reached him on the third day after that, and he began to read to our hushed little circle on the night of the fourth.

The written statement took up the tale at a point after it had, in a manner, begun. The fact to be in possession of was that his old friend, the youngest of several daughters of a country parson, had, at the age of twenty, come up to London, a bit anxiously, to answer an advertisement for a governess and private teacher for two small children.

This person who placed the advertisement proved, on her presenting herself at a house in Harley, a gentleman, a bachelor in the prime of life, such a figure as had never been seen, save in a dream or an old novel, by a fluttered, anxious girl out of a Hampshire vicarage.

One could easily fix his type; it never, happily, dies out. He was handsome, bold, and pleasant, off-hand, gay, and kind. He struck her as gallant and splendid, but what took her most and gave her courage was that he put the whole thing to her as a kind of favor, an obligation he would be grateful if she took on.

She saw him as rich, but fearfully extravagant—saw him all in a glow of high fashion, of good looks, of expensive habits, of charming ways with women. He had for his town residence, a big house filled with the spoils of travel and the trophies of the chase; but it was to his country home, an old family place in Essex, that he wished her to proceed.

He had been left, by the death of their parents in India, guardian to a small nephew and niece, children of a younger, military brother, whom he had lost two years before. These children were, for a man in his position—a man without the right sort of experience or patience—very heavily on his hands.

It had all been a great worry and, on his own part doubtless, but he pitied the poor chicks and had done all he could; had in particular sent them down to his other house, the proper place for them being of course the country, and kept them there, from the first, with the best people he could find to look after them.

The awkward thing was that they had practically no other relations and that his own affairs took up all his time. He had put them in possession of Bly, which was healthy and secure, and had placed at the head of their little establishment—but below stairs only—an excellent woman, Mrs. Grose, whom he was sure his visitor would like, and who had formerly been maid to his mother.

She was now house-keeper and was also for the time taking care of the little girl, of whom, without children of her own, she was, by good luck, extremely fond. There were plenty of people to help, but of course the young lady who should go down as governess would have full authority. She would also have, in holidays, to look after the small boy, who had been for a term at school—young as he was, but what else could be done?—and who, as the holidays were about to begin, would return any day.

There had been for the two children at first a young lady whom they had had the bad luck to lose. She had done for them quite beautifully—she was a most respectable person—till her death, the difficulties of which had left no alternative but school for little Miles.

Mrs. Grose, since then, in the way of manners and things, had done as she could for Flora; and there were, also, a cook, a house-maid, a dairy-woman, and an old gardener, all likewise respectable.

So far had Douglas presented his picture when someone asked, "And what did the former governess die of?—of too much respectability?"

Our friend's answer was prompt.

"That will come out. I don't anticipate."

"In her successor's place," I suggested, "I should have wished to learn if the office brought with it—"

"Any danger to life?" Douglas completed my thought. "She did wish to learn, and she did learn. You shall hear in due cause what she learned. Meanwhile, of course, the prospect struck her as slightly grim. She was young, untried, and nervous: it was a vision of serious duties and little company, of great loneliness.

"She hesitated—took a couple of days to consult and consider. But the salary offered much exceeded her modest measure, and on a second interview she faced the music, she engaged for the position."

Douglas, with this, paused, which moved me to throw in, "The moral of which is, of course, that she was led astray by the young man. She surrendered to his charm."

He got up and, as he had done the night before, went to the fire, gave a stir to a log with his foot, and then stood a moment with his back to us.

"She saw him only twice."

"Yes, but that's just the beauty of her passion."

"To my surprise, on this Douglas turned round to me.

"It WAS the beauty of it. There were others," he went on, "who hadn't given in to it. He told her frankly all his difficulty—that for several applicants the conditions had been too much. They were, somehow, simply afraid. It sounded dull—it sounded strange; and all the more so because of his main condition."

"Which was—?"

"That she should never trouble him—but never, never: neither appeal nor complain nor write about anything; only meet all questions herself, receive all moneys from his solicitor, take the whole thing over and let him alone.

"She promised to do this, and mentioned to me that when, with this problem lifted from him, he held her hand and thanked her for the sacrifice, she already felt rewarded."

"But was that all her reward?" one of the ladies asked.

"She never saw him again."

"Oh!" said the lady; which, as our friend immediately left us again, was the only other word of importance contributed to the subject till, the next night, by the corner of the fire, in the best chair, he opened the faded red cover of a thin old-fashioned gilt-edged album.

The whole thing took indeed more nights than one, but on the first occasion the same lady put another question.

"What is your title?"

"I haven't one."

"Oh, *I* have!" I said.

But Douglas, without heeding me, had begun to read with a fine clearness that was like giving to the ear the beauty of his author's hand the story the governess told.

I SPENT LONG hours in a coach that carried me to the stopping place at which I was to be met by a carriage from the house. This I found, toward the close of the June afternoon, to be waiting for me.

Driving at that hour, on a lovely day, through a country to which the summer sweetness seemed to offer me a friendly welcome, my courage mounted. I had expected something so terrible that what greeted me was a surprise. I remember as a most pleasant impression the broad, clear front of the house, its open windows and fresh curtains and a pair of maids looking out.

I remember the lawn and the bright flowers and the sound of my wheels on the gravel, and the trees over which the birds circled in the golden sky. The scene had a fineness that made it a different affair from my own small home, and there immediately appeared at the door, with a little girl in hand, a person who bowed to me as if I were the mistress of the house or a distinguished visitor.

I had received in Harley Street a narrower idea of the place, and that, as I recalled it, made me think the owner still more of a gentleman; it suggested that what I was to enjoy might be something beyond his promise.

The little girl who accompanied Mrs. Grose appeared to me a creature so charming as to make it a great fortune to have to do with her. She was the most beautiful child I had ever seen, and I afterward wondered that my employer had not told me more of her.

I slept little that first night—I was too much excited. The feeling added to my sense of the goodness with which I was treated. The large, impressive room, the great bed, the full draperies, the long looking-glass in which, for the first time, I saw myself from head to foot, all struck me—like the charm of my small charge—as so many things thrown in. It was thrown in as well, from the first moment, that I should get on with Mrs. Grose, a relation I fear I had rather worried about on the way there in the coach.

The only thing in this early outlook that might have made me shrink again was her being so glad to see me. I saw, within half an hour, that she was so glad—stout, simple, plain, clean, wholesome woman—as to be positively on her guard against showing it too much. I wondered why she should wish not to show it, and that, with suspicion, might of course have made me uneasy.

But it was a comfort that there could be no uneasiness in connection with anything so perfect as the little girl, the vision of whose beauty had probably more than anything else to do with the restlessness that, before morning, made me several times rise and wander about my room to take in the whole prospect; to watch from my open window the faint summer dawn, to look at such portions of the rest of the house as I could catch, and to listen, while in the fading dusk, the first birds began to stir, for the possible sound or two, less natural and not without but within, that I fancied I heard before I rose.

There had been a moment when I believed I heard, faint and far, the cry of a child; there had been another when I found myself starting as at the passage before my door of a light footstep. But these fancies were not marked enough not to be thrown off, and it is only in the light, or the gloom, I should rather say, of other and subsequent matters that they now come back to me. At present, to watch, to teach, to "form" little Flora would too evidently be the making of a happy and useful life.

It had been agreed between us downstairs that after this first occasion I should have her as a matter of course at night, her small white bed being already arranged to that end in my room. What I had undertaken was the whole care of her, and she had remained, just this last time, with Mrs. Grose, considering my strangeness and her natural timidity. In spite of this—which the child herself, in the oddest way, had been perfectly frank and brave about, admitting it without a sign of being uncomfortable, I felt quite sure she would soon like me.

It was part of what I already liked Mrs. Grose for, the pleasure I could see her feel in my admiring gaze as I sat at supper with four tall candles, and my pupil in a high chair and a bib, brightly facing me, between them. There were naturally things that in Flora's presence could pass between us only as gratified looks and obscure talk.

"And the little boy—does he look like her? Is he too so very remarkable?" I asked.

"Oh, miss, MOST remarkable. If you think well of this one!"—and she stood there with a plate in her hand, beaming at our companion, who looked from one of us to the other with good-natured, heavenly eyes that contained nothing to check us.

"Yes; if I do—?"

"You WILL be carried away by the little gentleman!"

"Well, that, I think, is what I came for—to be carried away. I'm afraid, however," I added, "I'm rather easily carried away. I was carried away in London!"

I can still see Mrs. Grose's broad face as she heard this.

"In Harley Street?"

"In Harley Street."

"Well, miss, you're not the first—and won't be the last."

"Oh, I can't imagine," I could laugh, "being the only one. My other pupil, I understand, returns tomorrow?"

"Not tomorrow—Friday, miss. He arrives, as you did, by the coach, and is to be met by the same carriage."

I immediately said that the proper, as well as the pleasant and friendly thing, would be, on the arrival of the coach, that I should be waiting for him with his little sister. Mrs. Grose agreed so heartily that I somehow took her manner as a kind of comforting pledge—never falsified, thank heaven!—that we should on every question be quite at one. Oh, she was glad I was there!

What I felt the next day was, I suppose, nothing that could be fairly called my reacting to the cheer of my arrival; it was probably at the most only a slight coming down from my high of the day before, produced by a fuller measure of the scale, as I walked round the house, gazed up at it, and took in, my new circumstances.

They had an extent and mass for which I had not been prepared, and in the presence of which I found myself a little scared as well as a little proud. Lessons, in this state I was in, certainly suffered a delay; I knew that my first duty was, by the gentlest arts, to win the child to the sense of knowing me.

I spent the day with her out-of-doors; I arranged with her, to her great satisfaction, that it should be she, she only, who might show me the place. She showed it step by step, room by room, and secret by secret, with funny, delightful, childish talk about it, with the result, in half an hour, of our becoming very close friends.

Young as she was, I was struck, throughout our little tour, with her confidence and courage, with the way, in empty chambers and dull corridors, on crooked stair-cases that made me pause, and even on the summit of an old square tower that made me dizzy, her desire to tell me so many more things than she asked me about.

I have not seen Bly since the day I left it, and I daresay that to my older and more informed eyes it would now appear smaller. But as my little guide, with her hair of gold and her frock of blue, danced before me round corners and down the hall-ways, I had the view of a castle of romance inhabited by a rosy sprite, such a place as would take all color out of story-books and fairy-tales.

Wasn't it just a story-book over which I had fallen asleep and been dreaming? No; it was just a big, ugly, antique house, with a few features of a building still older, half-replaced and half-used, in which I had the fancy of our being almost as lost as passengers in a great ship floating free. Well, I was, strangely, at the helm!

11

THIS CAME HOME to me when, two days later, I drove with Flora to meet the little gentleman; and all the more for an incident on the second evening that deeply upset me.

The first day had been, as I said, reassuring; but I was to see it wind up in uneasiness. The mail that evening contained a letter for me in the hand of my employer. I found to be composed but of a few words, enclosing another letter addressed to himself, its seal still unbroken.

"This, I recognize, is from the headmaster, and the headmaster's an awful bore," it said. "Read him, please; deal with him; but don't report. Not a word. I'm off!"

I broke the sea, took the unopened letter to my room, and only read it just before going to bed. I should have let it wait till morning, for it gave me a second sleepless night. With no one to advise me, the next day I was full of distress; and I decided to open myself to Mrs. Grose.

"What does it mean? The child's dismissed his school."

She gave me a look that I remarked at the moment; then, with a quick blankness seemed to take it back.

"But aren't they all—?"

"Sent home—yes. But only for the holidays. Miles may never go back at all."

She turned red.

"They won't take him?"

"They absolutely decline."

At this she raised her eyes, which she had turned from me; I saw them fill with tears.

"What has he done?"

I hesitated; then I judged it best simply to hand her my letter—which, however, had the effect of making her, without taking it, simply put her hands behind her.

She shook her head sadly.

"Such things are not for me, miss."

She couldn't read! I made up for my mistake as I could, and opened my letter again to repeat it to her; then, not sure it was the right thing to do, I folded it again and put it back in my pocket.

"Is he really BAD?"

The tears were still in her eyes.

"Do the gentlemen say so?"

"They go into no detail. They simply say they are sorry, but that it should be impossible to keep him. That can have only one meaning."

Mrs. Grose listened with quiet emotion; she didn't ask me what the meaning might be; so that, presently, to put the thing to her with some meaning, I went on:

"That he's an injury to the others."

At this, she got angry.

"Master Miles! HIM an injury?"

There was such a flood of good faith in it that, though I had not yet seen the child, my fears made me jump to how crazy the idea was. I found myself, to meet my friend the better, speaking to her in a humoring manner.

"To his poor little innocent mates!"

"It's too dreadful," cried Mrs. Grose, "to say such cruel things! Why, he's scarce ten years old."

"Yes, yes; it's not to be believed."

She was evidently grateful for such a statement.

"See him, miss, first. THEN believe it!"

I felt then a new desire to see him; it was the beginning of a curiosity that, for the next hours, was to deepen almost to pain. Mrs.

Grose, aware of what she had produced in me, followed it up with assurance.

"You might as well believe it of the little lady. Bless her," she added the next moment—"LOOK at her!"

I turned and saw that Flora, whom, ten minutes before I had established in the school-room with a sheet of white paper, a pencil, and a copy of nice "round o's," now presented herself to view at the open door.

She expressed in her way something far above simply my duties; she looked to me with a childish light that seemed a result of the affection she had developed for me, which had made it necessary that she should follow me. I needed nothing more than this to feel the full force of Mrs. Grose's comparison. Catching my pupil in my arms, I covered her with kisses, as if to make up for my lack of faith.

Nevertheless, the rest of the day I watched for a further occasion to approach my companion, especially as, toward evening, I began to fancy she was trying to avoid me. I overtook her on the stairs as we went down together, and at the bottom held her with my hand.

"I take what you said to me at noon as a declaration that YOU'VE never known him to be bad."

She threw back her head.

"Oh, never known him—I don't pretend THAT!"

I was upset again.

"Then you HAVE known him—?"

"Yes indeed, miss, thank God!"

On reflection I accepted this.

"You mean that a boy who never is—?"

"Is no boy for ME!"

I held her tighter.

"You like them with the spirit to be naughty?" Then, keeping pace with her, I answered, "So do I. But not to the degree to contaminate—"

"To contaminate?" My big word left her at a loss. I explained it. "To affect others with his badness."

She stared, taking my meaning in; but it produced in her an odd laugh.

"Are you afraid he'll contaminate YOU?"

She put the question with such a fine bold humor that, with a laugh to match her own, I gave way for the time being. But the next day, as the hour for my drive approached, I cropped up in another place.

"What was the lady who was here before?"

"The last governess? She was also young and pretty—almost as young and pretty, miss, as you."

"Ah, then, I hope her youth and her beauty helped her! He seems to like us young and pretty!"

"Oh, he DID," Mrs. Grose said. "It was the way he liked everyone!" She had no sooner said than she caught herself up. "I mean that's HIS way—the master's."

I was struck.

"But of whom did you speak first?"

She looked blank, but colored.

"Why, of HIM."

"Of the master?"

"Of who else?"

There was so obviously no one else that the next moment I lost my impression of her having accidentally said more than she meant; and I merely asked her what I wanted to know.

"Did SHE see anything in the boy—?"

"That wasn't right? She never told me."

"Was she careful—particular?"

Mrs. Grose appeared to try to be fair.

"About some things—yes."

"But not about all?"

Again she considered.

"Well, miss—she's gone. I won't tell tales."

"I quite understand," I quickly replied; but I thought it, after an instant, safe to go on:

"Did she die here?"

"No—she went off."

I don't know what there was in Mrs. Grose's response that struck me as not being completely open.

"Went off to die?"

Mrs. Grose looked out of the window, but I felt I had a right to know what young persons engaged for Bly were expected to do. So I continued.

"She was taken ill, you mean, and went home?"

"She was not taken ill, so far as appeared, in this house. She left it, at the end of the year to go home, as she said, for a short holiday, to which the time she had put in had certainly given her a right. We had at that time a young woman—a nursemaid who stayed on, who was a good girl and clever, and SHE took the children for the time being. But our young lady never came back, and at the moment I was expecting her I heard from the master that she was dead."

I turned this over.

"But of what?"

"He never told me! But please, miss," said Mrs. Grose, "I must get to my work."

III

HER TURNING HER back on me was not a snub that checked the growth of our friendship. We met, after I brought home little Miles, more intimately than ever on the ground of my utter lack of belief in the evil suggested of him. I thought it terrible that the child I now met should be considered to have a bad influence on other children.

I was a little late on the scene, and I felt, as he stood wistfully looking out for me before the door of the inn at which the coach had put him down, that I saw in him, on the instant, the same positive air of innocence I had, from the first moment, seen in his little sister.

He was unbelievably beautiful, and Mrs. Grose had put her finger on it: everything but a passion of tenderness for him was swept away by his presence. What I then and there took him to my heart for was something that I have never found to the same degree in any child—his air of knowing nothing in the world but love.

It would have been impossible to carry a bad name with a greater sweetness, and by the time I got back to Bly with him I was bewildered—so far, that is, as I was not outraged—by the sense of the terrible letter locked up in a drawer in my room. When I managed a private word with Mrs. Grose, I declared to her that it was terribly wrong. She understood me at once.

"You mean the cruel charge—?"

"It makes no sense. My dear woman, LOOK at him!"

She smiled at my having discovered his charm.

"I assure you, miss, I do nothing else! What will you say, then?" she asked.

"In answer to the letter?"

I had made up my mind.

"Nothing."

"And to his uncle?"

I was equally brief.

"Nothing."

"And to the boy himself?"

I was wonderful.

"Nothing."

"Then I'll stand by you. We'll see it out."

"We'll see it out!" I echoed, giving her my hand.

She held me there a moment, then asked, "Would you mind, miss, if I used the freedom—"

"To kiss me? No!"

After we had embraced like sisters, I felt still more her support. This, at all events, was for the time how we left it. It was a time so full that, as I recall it, it takes all the art I have to make it a little distinct. What I look back at with amazement is the situation I accepted. I had agreed, with my companion, to see it out, and I was under a charm that could smooth away any of the difficulties of such an effort. I was lifted on a wave of love and pity.

I found it simple, in my ignorance, my confusion, and perhaps my conceit, to assume that I could deal with a boy whose education was on the point of beginning. I can't even remember to this day what I proposed for the end of his holidays and the start, once again, of his studies. Lessons with me that charming summer we all assumed he was to have; but I now feel that, for weeks, the lessons must have been my own.

I learned something—at first, certainly—that had not been one of the teachings of my small, protected life; I learned to be amused, and not to think for the morrow. It was the first time, in a manner, that I had known space and air and freedom, all the music of summer and mystery of nature. But it was a trap—not designed, but deep—to whatever, in me, was most excitable.

The best way to picture it all is to say that I was off my guard. The children gave me so little trouble—they were of a gentleness so extra-ordinary. I used to wonder—but even this is dim—how the rough future (for all futures are rough!) would handle them and might bruise them.

They had the bloom of health and happiness; and yet, as if I had been in charge of a pair of little princes for whom everything, to be right, they would have to be enclosed and protected; the only form that, in my fancy, the after years could take for them was that of a romantic, royal extension of the garden and the park.

It may be, of course, that what suddenly broke into this gives the previous time a charm of stillness—that hush in which something gathers or crouches. The change was actually like the spring of a beast.

In the first weeks the days were long; they often, at their finest, gave me what I used to call my own hour, the hour when, for my pupils, tea-time and bed-time having come and gone, I had, before my own bed-time, a small interval alone. Much as I liked my companions, this hour was the thing in the day I liked most.

I liked it best of all when, as the light faded—or rather, I should say, the day lingered and the last calls of the birds sounded in a glowing sky from the old trees, I could take a turn in the grounds and enjoy, almost with a sense of property that amused and flattered me, the beauty and dignity of the place. It was a pleasure at these moments to feel myself at peace, and justly so, and also to reflect that by my wise decision, my quiet good sense, I was giving pleasure—if he ever thought of it!—to the one who had hired me.

What I was doing was what he had hoped and directly asked of me, and that I COULD, after all, do it proved even a greater joy than I had expected. I daresay I fancied myself, in short, a remarkable young woman, and took comfort in the faith that this would more publicly appear. Well, I needed to be remarkable to offer a front to the strange things that presently gave their first sign.

It was one afternoon in the middle of my hour: the children were tucked away, and I had come out for my stroll. One of the thoughts that used to be with me in these wanderings was that it would be as charming as a story suddenly to meet someone. Someone would appear at the turn of a path and would stand before me and smile and approve. I didn't ask more than that—I only asked that he should KNOW; and the only way to be sure he knew would be to see it in the light of his handsome face.

That was exactly present to me—by which I mean the face— when, on the first of these occasions, at the end of a long June day, I stopped short on emerging from one of the garden areas and came into view of the house. What arrested me on the spot—with a shock much greater than any vision had allowed for—was the sense that my imagination had, in a flash, turned real.

He did stand there!—but high up, beyond the lawn, at the top of the tower to which, on that first morning, little Flora had taken me. This tower was one of a pair—square, out of place—that were at opposite ends of the house, and were probably absurdities, saved in a measure by not being wholly separate from the house, nor of a height too pretentious, dating from a romantic revival that was already part of the past.

I admired them, had fancies about them, for we could all profit in a degree, especially when they loomed through the dusk, by the grandeur of them. Yet it was not at such an elevation that the figure I had so often invoked seemed most in place. It produced in me, this figure in the clear twilight, two distinct gasps of emotion which were, sharply, the shock of my first, and then my second surprise. My second was the mistake of my first: the man who met my eyes was not the person I had supposed.

There came to me thus a vision of which, after these years, there is no living view that I can hope to give. An unknown man in a lonely place is a permitted object of fear to a young woman privately bred; and the figure that faced me was—a few more seconds assured me—as little anyone I knew as it was the image that had been in my mind. I had not seen it in Harley Street—I had not seen it anywhere. The place, moreover, in the strangest way, had, on the instant, and by the very fact of its appearance, become something only I saw.

To me at least, making my statement here with a thoughtfulness with which I have never before made it, the whole feeling of the moment returns. It was as if, while I took in—what I did take in—all the rest of the scene was a blank. I can hear again, as I write, the hush in which the sounds of evening dropped. The birds stopped their sounds in the golden sky, and the friendly hour lost, for the minute, all its voice.

But there was no other change in nature. The gold was still in the sky, the clearness in the air, and the man who looked at me from the tower was as definite as a picture in a frame. That's how I thought, with great quickness, of each person he might be and was not. We saw each other across the distance quite long enough for me to ask myself who, then, he was, and to feel, as a result of my inability to say, a wonder that became very strong.

The great question, or one of them, is, afterward, I know with regard to certain matters, how long they lasted. Well, this matter of mine, think what you will of it, lasted while I caught at a dozen possibilities, none of which made a difference for the better, that I could see, in there having been in the house—and for how long?—a person who was a complete stranger to me.

It lasted while I felt a little anger with the sense that my office demanded that there should be no such ignorance and no such person. It lasted while this person—and there was a touch of a strange freedom in the sign of familiarity of his wearing no hat—seemed to fix me, from his position, with just the question, through the fading light, that his own presence stirred up.

We were too far apart to call to each other, but there was a moment at which, at shorter range, some challenge between us would have been the right result of our mutual stare. He was in one of the angles of the tower, the one away from the house, standing very erect, with both hands on the railing. But after a minute, as if to add to the viewing, he slowly changed his place—passed, looking at me all the while, to the opposite corner of the tower. During this time he never took his eyes from me, and I can see at this moment the way his hand, as he went, passed from one post to the next.

He stopped at the other corner, but not for long. Turning away, he still fixed me. That was all I knew.

IV

IT WAS NOT that I didn't wait for more to happen, for I was rooted as deeply as I was shaken. Was there a "secret" at Bly—an insane, not mentioned relative kept locked up somewhere? I can't say how long I turned it over, or how long, in my curiosity and dread, I remained where I was. I only recall that when I entered the house again darkness had closed in.

The strong emotions I felt had held me and driven me, for I must, in circling about the place, have walked three miles; but I was to be, later on, so much more overwhelmed, that this mere dawn of alarm was still but a human chill. The oddest part of it was the part I played in the hall on meeting Mrs. Grose.

This picture comes back to me—the impression I received on my return, of the wide white paneled space, bright in the lamplight, with its portraits and red carpet, and of the surprised look of my friend, which told me she had missed me. It came to me that, with her heartiness, and her relief at seeing me, she knew nothing whatever that could bear upon the incident I was ready to tell her about. I had not expected that her comfortable face would pull me up, and I somehow measured the importance of what I had seen, hesitating, finally, to mention it.

Scarce anything in the whole history seems to me so odd as that my real beginning of fear was one, as I may say, with the instinct of sparing my companion. In the pleasant hall, with her eyes on me, I, for a reason I couldn't have put into words, made a decision not to tell her what I had experienced. I gave her a vague reason for being late and, with the plea of the beauty of the night and of the heavy dew and wet feet, I went to my room.

Here it was another affair, odd enough. There were hours, from day to day—or at least there were moments, snatched from my duties—when I had to shut myself up to think. It was not so much that I was more nervous than I could bear to be, as that I was afraid of becoming so; for the truth I had now to turn over was, simply and clearly, the truth that I could arrive at no account whatever of the visitor I had so unexpectedly seen.

It took a little time to see how I could speak without stirring up questions or domestic complications. The shock I suffered must have sharpened my senses; I felt sure, at the end of three days, as the result of closer attention, that I had not been practiced upon by the servants, nor made the object of any "game."

Of whatever it was I knew, nothing was known around me. There was but one sane way it could be explained: someone had taken a liberty rather gross. That was what I said to myself. Some traveler, curious about old houses, had made his way in unobserved, enjoyed the prospect from the best point of view, and then stolen out as he came. If he had given me such a bold stare, that was but part of his daring. The good thing, after all, was that we should surely see no more of him.

This was not so good a thing, I admit, as not to leave me to judge that what, essentially, made nothing else mean much, was simply my own charming work. My charming work was my life with Miles and Flora, and through nothing could I so like it as through feeling that I could throw myself into it in trouble.

The attraction of my small charges was a constant joy, leading me to wonder at the vanity of my original fears, the distaste I had begun with for the probable gray prose of my office. There was to be no gray prose, it appeared, and no long grind; so how could work not be charming that presented itself as daily beauty? It was all the romance of the nursery and poetry of the school-room. I can express in no other way the interest my companions inspired in me. How can I describe it except by saying that instead of growing used to them—and it's a marvel for a governess!—I made constant fresh discoveries.

There was one direction, however, in which these discoveries stopped: deep obscurity continued to cover the report of the boy's conduct at school. It had been given me, as I have noted, the decision to face that mystery without a pang. Perhaps even it would be nearer the truth to say that—without a word—Miles himself had cleared it up. He had made the whole charge absurd.

My conclusion bloomed with the reality of his innocence: he was only too fine and fair for the ugly, not- clean school world, and he had paid a price for it. I reflected that the sense of such differences, such superiorities of quality, always, on the part of the majority—which could include even stupid head-masters—would turn always to the hateful.

Both the children had a gentleness that kept them—how shall I express it?—almost impersonal, and certainly not deserving to be punished. I remember feeling, with regard to Miles especially, as if he had, as it were, no history. We expect it of a small child, but there was in this beautiful little boy something very sensitive, yet happy, that, more than in any creature of his age I have ever seen, struck me as beginning fresh each day.

He had never for a second suffered. I took this as proof of his having never really been corrected. If he had been wicked he would have "caught" it, and I should have found a trace if it. I found nothing, and he was therefore an angel. He never spoke of his school, never mentioned a friend or a master; and I, for my part, was quite too much disgusted with the school to bring them up.

Of course I was under his spell, and the wonderful part is that, even at the time, I knew it. But I gave myself up to it; it was a cure for any pain, and I had more pains than one. I was in receipt in these days of disturbing letters from home, where things were not going well. But with my children, what things in the world mattered? I was too much taken up by their loveliness.

There was a Sunday—to get on with my story—when it rained with such force and for so many hours that there could be no thought of going to church; as a result, I arranged with Mrs. Grose that, should the evening show improvement, we would attend together the late service.

The rain happily stopped, and I prepared for our walk, which, through the park and by the road to the village, would be a matter of twenty minutes. Coming down the stairs to meet Mrs. Grose in the hall, I remembered a pair of gloves that had required three stitches and that had received them while I sat with the children at their tea, served on Sundays, by exception, in that cold, clean temple, the "grown-up" dining room. The gloves had been dropped there, and I turned to recover them.

The day was gray enough, but the afternoon light still lingered, and it enabled me, on crossing the threshold, not only to recognize, on a chair near the wide window, then closed, the articles I wanted, but to become aware of a person on the other side of the window looking in.

One step into the room was enough; my vision was instantly there. The person looking in was the person who had already appeared to me. He appeared again with, I won't say greater distinctness, for that was impossible, but with a nearness that represented a forward stride in our relations and made me, as I met him, catch my breath and turn cold.

He was the same—and seen, this time, as he had been seen before, from the waist up, the window not going down to the terrace on which he stood. His face was close to the glass, yet the effect of this better view was, strangely, only to show me how intense the former had been. He remained but a few seconds—long enough to convince me he also saw and recognized me.

It was as if I had been looking at him for years and had known him always. But something, however, happened this time that had not happened before; his stare into my face, through the glass and across the room, was as deep and hard as then, but it quitted me for a moment during which I could still see it look at other things in the room.

There came to me the added shock of the certainty that it was not for me he had come there. He had come for someone else. This flash of this knowledge—for it was knowledge in the midst of dread—produced in me the strangest effect; I felt, as I stood there, a sudden sense of duty and courage. I bounded out of the door again, reached that of the house, got, in an instant, upon the drive, and, passing along the terrace as fast as I could, turned a corner and came full in sight.

But it was in sight of nothing—my visitor was gone. I stopped, I almost dropped, with relief, but I took in the whole scene—I gave him time to appear again. I call it time, but how long was it? I can't speak today of the time of these things. That kind of measure must have left me: they couldn't have lasted as long as they seemed to last.

The terrace and the whole place, the lawn and the garden beyond it, all I could see of the park, were empty with a great emptiness. There were shrubberies and big trees, but I remember the clear assurance I felt that none of them concealed him. He was there or was not there if I didn't see him.

I got hold of this; then, instead of returning as I had come, I went to the window. It came to me that I ought to place myself where he had stood. I did so; I applied my face to the pane and looked, as he had looked, into the room. As if, at this moment, to show me exactly what his range had been, Mrs. Grose, as I had done for himself just before, came in from the hall.

With this I had the full image of what had already occurred. She saw me as I had seen my own visitor; she pulled up short as I had done; I gave her something of the shock that I had received. She turned white, and this made me ask myself if I, too, had paled. She stared, and then retreated on just MY lines, and I knew she had then passed out and come round to me and that I should presently meet her. I remained where I was, and while I waited thought of more things than one. But there's only one I mention: I wondered why SHE should be scared.

V

Oh, she let me know as soon as, round the corner of the house, she loomed again into view.

"What in the name of goodness is the matter—?"

She was flushed and out of breath.

I said nothing till she came quite near.

"With me?" I must have made a face. "Do I show it?"

"You're as white as a sheet. You look awful."

My need to respect the innocence of Mrs. Grose had dropped quietly from my shoulders, and if I wavered for an instant it was not with what I kept back. I put out my hand and she took it; I held her hard, liking to feel her close to me. There was a kind of support in her surprise.

"You came for me for church, but I can't go."

"Has anything happened?"

"Yes. You must know now. Did I look very queer?"

"Through this window? Dreadful!"

"Well," I said, "I've been frightened."

Mrs. Grose's eyes expressed plainly that SHE had no wish to be, yet she knew too well her place not to be ready to share. It was quite settled that she MUST share!

"What you saw from the dining room a minute ago was what *I* saw—just before—but it was much worse."

Her hand tightened.

"What was it?"

"A very odd man. Looking in."

"What odd man?"

"I haven't the least idea."

Mrs. Grose gazed round in vain.

"Where is he gone?"

"I know still less."

"Have you seen him before?"

"Yes—once. On the old tower."

She looked at me harder.

"Do you mean he's a stranger?"

"Oh, very much!"

"Yet you didn't tell me?"

"No—for reasons. But now that you've guessed—"

Mrs. Grose's round eyes met this charge.

"Ah, I haven't guessed!" she said... "How can I if YOU don't imagine?"

"I don't in the very least."

"You've seen him nowhere but on the tower?"

"And on this spot just now."

Mrs. Grose looked round again.

"What was he doing on the tower?"

"Only standing there looking down at me."

She thought a minute.

"Was he a gentleman?"

I found I had no need to think.

"No." She gazed in deeper wonder. "No."

"Nobody about the place? Nobody from the village?"

"Nobody—nobody. I didn't tell you, but I made sure."

She breathed a relief: this was, oddly, so much to the good, though it only went a little way.

"But if he isn't a gentleman—"

"What IS he? He's a terror."

"A terror?"

"He's—God help me if I know WHAT he is!"

Mrs. Grose looked round once more. She fixed her eyes on the darker distance, then, pulling herself together, turned to me with a change of subject.

"It's time we should be at church."

"Oh, I'm not fit for church!"

"Won't it do you good?"

"It won't do THEM—!"

I nodded at the house.

"The children?"

"I can't leave them now."

"You're afraid—?"

I spoke boldly.

"I'm afraid of HIM."

Mrs. Grose's large face showed for the first time the faint glimmer of something sharper. I made out in it the delayed dawn of an idea I had not given her, and it was as yet obscure to me. It comes back to me that I thought instantly of this as something I could get from her; and I felt it to be connected with the desire she presently showed to know more.

"When was it—on the tower?"

"About the middle of the month. At this same hour."

"Almost at dark," said Mrs. Grose.

"Oh, no, not nearly. I saw him as I see you."

"Then how did he get in?"

"And how did he get out?" I laughed. "I had no opportunity to ask him! This evening, you see, I went after him, he has not been able to get in."

"He only looks?"

"I hope it will be kept to that!" She let go my hand and turned away. I waited an instant, then I brought out, "Go to church. I must watch."

Slowly she faced me again.

"Do you fear for them?"

We met in another long look.

"Don't YOU?" Instead of answering she came nearer to the window and, for a minute, put her face to the glass. "You see how he could see," I meanwhile went on.

She didn't move.

"How long was he here?"

"Till I came out. I came to meet him."

Mrs. Grose turned round, and there was still more in her face.

"*I* couldn't have come out."

"Neither could I!" I laughed again. "But I did. I have my duty."

"So have I mine," she replied; after which she added: "What is he like?"

"I've been dying to tell you. But he's like nobody."

"Nobody?" she echoed.

"He has no hat." Then seeing in her face that she already, in this, with a deeper dismay, found a touch of a picture, I quickly added stroke to stroke. "He has red hair, very red, close-curling, and a pale face, long in shape, with straight, good features and little, rather queer whiskers that are as red as his hair. His eyebrows are somehow darker; they look arched. His eyes are sharp, strange—awful; but I only know clearly that they're rather small and very fixed. His mouth's wide, and his lips are thin, and except for his little whiskers he's quite clean-shaven. He made me feel as if he were an actor."

"An actor!"

"I've never seen one, but so I suppose them. He's tall, active, erect," I continued, "but never!—a gentleman."

My companion's face turned white as I went on; her round eyes started and her mouth gaped.

"A gentleman?" she cried, shocked: "He was never a gentleman!"

"You know him then?"

She tried to hold herself back.

"But he IS handsome?" I asked, trying to help her.

"Quite so!"

"And dressed—?"

"In somebody's clothes. They're smart, but not his own." She broke into a groan, "They're the master's!"

I caught it up.

"You DO know him?"

She faltered but a second.

"Quint!" she cried.

"Quint?"

"Peter Quint—his man, his valet, when he was here!"

"When the master was?"

Gaping still, but meeting me, she pieced it all together.

"He never wore his hat, but he did wear—well, there were waistcoats missed. They were both here—last year. Then the master went, and Quint was alone."

I followed, but halting a little.

"Alone?"

"Alone with US." Then, as from a deeper depth, "In charge," she added.

"And what became of him?"

She hung fire so long that I was still more mystified.

"He went, too," she brought out at last.

"Went where?"

Her expression, at this, became very strange.

"God knows where! He died."

"Died?" I almost shrieked.

She seemed to square herself, plant herself more firmly to utter the wonder of it.

"Yes. Mr. Quint is dead."

VI

IT TOOK OF course more than that exchange to place us together
in the presence of what we had now to live with—my tendency
to impressions of the order just experienced, and my companion's
knowledge, half concern and half pity, of it. There had been, this
evening after the shock left me, no attendance on any service but a
little service of tears and vows, of prayers and promises, a climax to
our retreating to the school-room and shutting ourselves up there to
have everything out.

The result of our having everything out was simply to reduce our
situation to the last of its elements. She herself had seen nothing, not
a shadow of a shadow, and nobody in the house had seen anything;
yet she accepted, without doubting my sanity, the truth as I gave it to
her, and she ended by showing me a tenderness of which the breath
has stayed with me as the sweetest of human characters.

What was settled between us was that we might bear things
together; and I was not even sure, in spite of her not seeing such
things, it was she who had the best of the burden. I knew then, as
well as later, what I was capable of doing to shelter my pupils; but
it took me some time to be wholly sure of what my companion was
prepared for.

I was odd company enough—quite as odd as the company I
received; but as I go over what we went through I see how much
common ground we must have found in the idea that, by good
fortune, COULD steady us. It was the idea that led me out of my

inner fear. I recall the way strength came to me before we separated for the night. We had gone over everything I had seen.

"He was looking for someone else, you say—someone who was not you?" she asked.

"He was looking for little Miles." A clearness now possessed me. "THAT'S whom he was looking for."

"But how do you know?"

"I know, I know, I know!" I grew more excited. "And YOU know, too, my dear!"

She didn't deny this, but resumed in a moment.

"What if HE should see him?"

"Little Miles? That's what he wants!"

She looked very scared again.

"The child?"

"Heaven forbid! He wants to appear to THEM."

That was a terrible idea, and yet, somehow, I could keep it at bay; which, moreover, as we lingered there, was what I succeeded in proving. I was certain I should see again what I had already seen, but something within me said that by offering myself bravely as the sole subject of such experience, by accepting, by inviting, by over-coming it, I should serve as a victim instead of them, and guard their peace and safety.

The last thing I said that night to Mrs. Grose was, "It strikes me that my pupils have never mentioned—"

She looked at me hard.

"The time they were here, and he with him?"

"The time they were with him, and his name, his presence, his history, in any way."

"The girl doesn't remember. She never heard or knew."

"Perhaps not. But Miles would remember—Miles would know."

"Ah, don't try him!" broke from Mrs. Grose.

I returned the look she had given me.

"Don't be afraid." I continued. "It IS rather odd."

"That he has never spoken of him?"

"Never by the least word. You say they were friends'?"

"Oh, it wasn't HIM!" Mrs. Grose said. "It was Quint's own fancy. To play with him, I mean—to spoil him." She paused, and then added, "Quint was much too free."

This gave me, straight from my vision of his face—SUCH a face!—a sudden sickness of disgust.

"Too free with MY boy?"

"Too free with everyone!"

I didn't, for the moment, think further of this than by the thought that part of it applied to several members of the household, of the half-dozen maids and men who were still of our small colony. But there was everything, for our anxiety, in the lucky fact that no uncomfortable legend, nothing to upset the servants, had ever, within anyone's memory, attached to the old place.

It had neither a bad name nor ill fame, and Mrs. Grose, apparently, only desired to cling to me and to be afraid in silence. I even put her, the very last thing, to the test. It was when, at midnight, she had her hand on the school-room door to take leave.

"I have it from you then—for it's of great importance—that he was definitely and admittedly bad?"

"Oh, not admittedly. *I* knew it—but the master didn't."

"And you never told him?"

"Well, he didn't like our telling such things—he hated complaints. He was terribly short with anything of that kind, and if people were all right to HIM—"

"He wouldn't be bothered with more?"

This squared well enough with my impression of him: he was not a trouble-loving gentleman, nor so very particular perhaps about some of the company HE kept.

All the same, I pressed my companion.

"I promise you *I* would have told!"

She felt my saying this.

"I daresay I was wrong. But, really, I was afraid."

"Afraid of what?"

"Of things that man could do. Quint was so clever."

I took this in more than, probably, I showed.

"You weren't afraid of—of his effect—?"

"His effect?" she repeated with a face of pain.

"On innocent little lives. They were in your charge."

"No, they were not in mine!" she returned. "The master believed in him and placed him here because he was supposed not to be well and the country air good for him. So he had everything to say. Yes—even about THEM."

"Them—that creature?" I had to smother a kind of howl. "And you could bear it!"

"No. I couldn't—and I can't now!"

And the poor woman burst into tears.

A rigid control, from the next day, was, as I have said, to follow on our emotions; yet how often and how passionately, for a week, we came back to the subject! Much as we had discussed it that Sunday night, I was, in the later hours especially, still haunted with the shadow of something she had not told me. I myself had kept back nothing, but there was a word Mrs. Grose had kept back.

I was sure, moreover, by morning, that this was not from a failure of frankness, but because on every side there were fears. It seems to me that by the time the morrow's sun was high I had restlessly read into the facts before us almost all the meaning they were to receive from subsequent and more cruel happenings.

What they gave me above all was the sinister figure of the living man—the dead one would keep awhile!—and of the months he had passed at Bly which, added up, made a great stretch. The limit of this evil time had arrived only when, on the dawn of a winter's morning, Peter Quint was found, by a laborer going to work, dead on the road from the village.

It was a death explained by a wound to his head; such a wound as might have been produced—and as, on the final evidence, HAD been—by a fatal slip in the dark after leaving the public house, on the steep icy slope, a wrong path, at the bottom of which he lay. The icy slope, the turn mistaken at night and in liquor, accounted, in the end, for everything; but there had been matters in his life—strange doings and perils, secret disorders, vices more than suspected—that would have accounted for a good deal more.

I scarce know how to put my story into words that shall be believed of my state of mind; but I was in these days able to find a joy in the very heroism the occasion demanded of me. I now saw that I had been asked for a service both admirable and difficult; and there would be a greatness in letting it be seen—in the right quarter!—that I could succeed where another might have failed.

It was a great help to me—I confess I rather applaud myself as I look back!—that I saw my service so strongly and so simply. I was there to protect and defend the little creatures, the most bereaved and most lovable in the world, the appeal of whose helplessness had suddenly become only too clear a deep, constant ache of one's own faithful heart. We were cut off, really, together; we were united in our danger. They had nothing but me, and I—well, I had THEM.

It was in short a magnificent chance. This chance presented itself to me in an image richly material. I was a screen—I was to stand before them. The more I saw, the less they would. I began to watch them in quiet suspense, a disguised excitement that might well, had it continued too long, have turned to something like madness. What saved me, I now see, was that it turned to something else altogether. It didn't last as suspense—it was replaced by terrible proofs, from the moment I took hold.

This moment dated from an afternoon hour I happened to spend in the grounds with the younger of my pupils. We had left Miles indoors on the red cushion of a deep window seat; he had wished to finish a book, and I was glad to encourage him. His sister, on the other hand, wanted to come out, and I strolled with her half an hour, seeking shade, for the sun was still high, the day warm.

I was reminded again, as we went, of how, like her brother, she made every effort—it was the charming thing in both of them—to let me alone without appearing to drop me, and to accompany me without appearing to surround me. They never begged me to say or do things. My attention to them really went to seeing them amuse themselves without me.

This was something for which they seemed actively to prepare, and that engaged me only as an active admirer. I walked in a world of their invention—they had no occasion whatever to draw upon mine; so that my time was taken only with being, for them, some remarkable person or thing that the game of the moment required, and that made for a happy and highly exceptional job.

I forget what I was supposed to be on the present occasion; I only remember that I was something very important and very quiet, and that Flora was playing very hard. We were on the edge of the lake, and, as we had lately begun geography, the lake was the Sea of Azof.

Suddenly, in these circumstances, I became aware that, on the other side, we had an interested viewer. The way this knowledge gathered in me was the strangest thing in the world—the strangest, that is, except in the very much stranger way the viewer so quickly appeared.

I sat with a piece of work—for it was something that could be done sitting—on the old stone bench which overlooked the pond; and in this position I began to take in with certainty, yet without direct vision, the presence at a distance of a third person.

The old trees, the thick shrubbery, made a great and pleasant shade, but it was all lit with the brightness of the hot, still hour. There was no lack of clearness in anything; none whatever, at least, in the belief I found myself forming as to what I saw straight before me and across the lake as a result of raising my eyes.

They were focused at this point on the stitching in which I was engaged, and I can feel once more the effort I made not to move them till I should so have steadied myself as to be able to make up my mind what to do. There was an alien object in view—a figure whose right of presence I instantly, fiercely questioned.

I remember counting over the possibilities, reminding myself that nothing was more natural, for instance, than the appearance of one of the men about the place, or of a messenger, a postman, or a boy from the village. That reminder had as little effect on my practical certainty—still without looking—as of its having upon the character and attitude of our visitor.

Of the positive identity of the person I saw I would assure myself as soon as the small clock of my courage should have ticked out the right second; meanwhile, with an effort that was already sharp enough, I moved my eyes to little Flora, who was about ten yards away.

My heart stood still for an instant with the wonder and terror of the question whether she too would see. I waited for what a cry from her, a sudden, innocent sign, either of interest or alarm, would tell me. I waited, but nothing came. There is something more fearful in this, I feel, than in anything I have to tell.

In the first place, I was struck by a sense that, within a minute, all sounds from her had dropped; and, in the second, by the circumstance that, also within the minute, she had, in her play, turned her back to the water. This was her attitude when I at last looked at her—looked with the conviction that we were still, together, under direct personal notice.

She had picked up a small flat piece of wood, which happened to have in it a little hole that evidently suggested to her the idea of sticking in another fragment that might figure as a mast, and make the thing a boat. This second piece, as I watched her, she was very intently attempting to tighten in its place.

My concern with what she was doing occupied me, so that after some seconds I felt I was ready for more. Then I again shifted my eyes—I faced what I had to face.

VII

I GOT HOLD of Mrs. Grose as soon after this as I could; I still hear myself cry as I threw myself into her arms, "They KNOW—it's too monstrous: they know!"

"What on earth—?"

I felt her inability to believe it as she held me.

"All that WE know—and heaven knows what else!" Then, as she let me go, I made it out to her. "Two hours ago in the garden"—I could scarce speak—"Flora SAW!"

Mrs. Grose took it as she might have taken a blow.

"She has told you?" she cried.

"Not a word—that's the horror. She kept it to herself! The child of eight, THAT child!"

I was shocked, but Mrs. Grose was more so.

"Then how do you know?"

"I was there—I saw, saw that she was perfectly aware."

"Do you mean aware of HIM?"

"No—of HER." I saw my feelings reflected in Mrs. Grose's face. "Another person this time, but quite as evil: a woman in black, pale and terrible—with such an air also, and such a face!—on the other side of the lake. I was there with the child—and she came."

"Came how—from where?"

"From where they come from! She just appeared and stood there—but not so near."

"And without coming nearer?"

"For the effect, she might have been as close as you!"

My friend, with an odd movement, fell back a step.

"Was she someone you've never seen?"

"Yes. But someone the child has. Someone YOU have." Then, to show I had thought it all out, I said, "The governess—the one who died."

"Miss Jessel?"

"Miss Jessel. You don't believe me?"

She turned right and left in her troubled feelings.

"How can you be sure?"

This drew from me, in the state of my nerves, a flash of anger. "Then ask Flora—SHE'S sure!" But I had no sooner spoken than I caught myself. "No, for God's sake, DON'T! She'll say she isn't—she'll lie!"

Mrs. Grose was not too upset to protest.

"Ah, how CAN you say that?"

"Because I'm clear. Flora doesn't want me to know."

"It's only to spare you."

"No, no—there are depths! The more I go over it, the more I see in it, and the more I see in it, the more I fear. I don't know what I DON'T see—what I DON'T fear!"

Mrs. Grose tried to keep up with me.

"You mean you're afraid of seeing her again?"

"Oh, no; that's nothing—now! It's of NOT seeing her."

But my companion only looked pale.

"I don't understand you."

"Why, it's that the child may keep it up—and that she certainly WILL—without my knowing it."

At this Mrs. Grose broke down, yet soon pulled herself together again as if from the sense of what, should we yield an inch, there would really be to give way to.

"Dear, we must keep our heads! After all, if she doesn't mind—!" It was a grim joke. "Maybe she likes it!"

"Likes SUCH things—a scrap of an infant!"

"Isn't it just a proof of her blessed innocence?" my friend bravely asked.

She brought me, for the instant, almost round.

"Oh, we must clutch at THAT—we must cling to it! If it isn't a proof of what you say, it's a proof of—God knows what! For the woman's a horror of horrors."

Mrs. Grose, at this, fixed her eyes on the ground; then, raising them, said, "Tell me how you know."

"Then you admit it's what she was?" I cried.

"Tell me how you know," my friend repeated.

"Know? By seeing her! By the way she looked."

"At you, do you mean—so wickedly?"

"Dear me, no—I could have borne that. She gave me never a glance. She only fixed her eyes on the child."

Mrs. Grose tried to see it.

"Fixed her?"

"With such awful eyes!"

She stared at mine as if they might resemble them.

"Do you mean of dislike?"

"God help us, no. Of something much worse."

"Worse than dislike?"

This left her indeed at a loss.

"With a determined look, a kind of fury of intention."

I made her turn pale.

"Intention?"

"To get hold of her." Mrs. Grose, her eyes lingering on mine, gave a shudder and walked to the window; and while she stood there looking out I completed my statement. "THAT'S what Flora knows."

After a little she turned round.

"The person was in black, you say?"

"In mourning—rather poor, almost shabby. But—yes—with great beauty."

I now saw to what I had brought her, for she visibly weighed this.

"Oh, handsome—very, very," I insisted; "wonderfully handsome. But evil"

She slowly came back to me.

"Miss Jessel—WAS evil."

She once more took my hand in both her own, holding it tight as if to fortify me against the alarm I might draw from this disclosure.

"They were both evil," she finally said.

For a little we faced it once more together; and I found a degree of help in seeing it now so straight.

"I'm grateful," I said, "for the great decency of your not having spoken before this; but the time has certainly come to give me the whole thing." She appeared to agree to this, but still only in silence; seeing which I went on.

"I must have it now. Of what did she die? Come, there was something between them."

"There was everything."

"In spite of the difference—?"

"Of their rank,"—she said. "SHE was a lady."

I turned it over; I again saw.

"Yes—she was a lady."

"And he so dreadfully below her," said Mrs. Grose.

I felt I needn't press too hard on the place of a servant in the scale of things; but there was nothing to prevent an acceptance of my companion's measure of Miss Jessel's fall in social standing. There was a way to deal with that, and I dealt the more readily for my vision of our employer's late clever, good-looking man; he was impudent, assured, spoiled, depraved.

"The fellow was a dog."

Mrs. Grose considered this.

"I've never seen one like him. He did what he wished."

"With HER?"

"With them all."

It was as if now, in my friend's eyes, Miss Jessel had again appeared. I seemed for an instant to see them, as distinctly as I had seen her by the pond; and I brought out, "It must have been also what SHE wished!"

Mrs. Grose's face showed it had been indeed, but she said at the same time, "Poor woman—she paid for it!"

"Then you do know what she died of?" I asked.

"No—I know nothing. I wanted not to know; I was glad I didn't; I thanked heaven she was well out of this!"

"Yet you had, then, your idea—"

"Of her real reason for leaving? Oh, yes—she couldn't have stayed. Fancy her—for a governess! And afterward I imagined—and what I imagine still is terrible."

"Not so terrible as what *I* do," I replied; on which I must have shown her a face of unhappy defeat. It brought out again all her pity for me, and at the touch of her kindness my power to resist broke down.

I burst into tears; she took me to her motherly breast, and my tears over-flowed.

"I don't do it!" I sobbed in despair; "I don't save or shield them! It's far worse than I dreamed—they're lost!"

VIII

WHAT I SAID to Mrs. Grose was true enough: there were in the matter I had put before her depths that I lacked the courage to sound; so that when we met once more, we were of a common mind about the duty of resistance to extravagant fancies. We were to keep our heads if we should do nothing else—difficult as that might be.

Late that night, while the house slept, we had another talk in my room, when she agreed with me as to its being beyond doubt that I had seen exactly what I had seen. To hold her to that, I had only to ask her how, if I made it up, I was able to give, of each of the persons appearing to me, a picture disclosing, to the last detail, their special marks—which made her instantly recognize them.

She wished of course—small blame to her!—to sink the whole subject; and I was quick to tell her that my own interest in it had taken the form of the way to escape from it. I met her on the ground of it being probable that when it occurred again—we took that for granted—I should get used to my danger, and that my personal danger had become the least of my worries. It was my new suspicion we couldn't bear; and yet even to this the later hours of the day brought little ease.

On leaving her after my first out-break, I returned to my pupils, associating the right cure for my fear with the sense of their charm, which I had already found to be a thing I could encourage, and which had never failed me. I simply, in other words, plunged into Flora's society, and there become aware—it was almost a luxury!—that she could put her little hand straight upon the spot that ached.

She looked at me in sweet wonder, and accused me to my face of having "cried." I thought I had brushed away the ugly signs: but I could—for the time—be glad they had not entirely disappeared. To gaze into the blue depths of the child's eyes and call their loveliness a trick was to be guilty of a great lack of trust. I couldn't give it up by merely wanting to, but I could repeat to Mrs. Grose—as I did over and over—that, with their voices in the air, their pressure on one's heart, and their faces against one's cheek, everything fell to the ground but their innocence.

It was a pity that, to settle this once for all, I had to go over again the signs of evil that, in the afternoon by the lake, had made a miracle of my show of self-possession. It was a pity to think again about the certainty of the moment itself, and how it had come to me as a reality that the connection I then surprised was a matter, for either party, of habit.

It was a pity I should have had to think out again the reasons for not having so much as questioned that the little girl saw our visitant even as I did, and that she wanted, by just so much as she did see, to make me suppose she didn't, at the same time, without showing anything, arrive at a guess as to whether I myself did! It was a pity I needed once more to describe the activity by which she sought to divert my attention—the increase of movement, the greater intensity of play, the singing and talk of nonsense.

Yet if I had not indulged, to prove there was nothing in it, in this review, I should have missed the two or three dim elements of comfort that still remained to me. I should not for instance have been able to insist to my friend that I was certain—which was so much to the good—that *I* at least had not betrayed myself. I should not have been pushed by my stress or desperation—I scarce know what to call it—to call such further aid to intelligence as might come from pushing my companion to the wall.

She had told me, bit by bit, under pressure, a great deal; but a small shifty spot on the wrong side of it all still sometimes brushed my mind, and I remember how on this occasion—the sleeping house, the sense of our danger and our watch seemed to help—I felt the importance of giving the last pull to the curtain.

"I don't believe anything so terrible," I remember saying. "No, let us put it definitely, my dear, that I don't. But if I did, you know, there's something I need, without sparing you the least bit more to get out of you. What was it you had in mind when, in our distress, before Miles came back, over the letter from his school, you said, under my insistence, that you didn't pretend he had not EVER been 'bad'? He has NOT 'ever,' in these weeks that I have lived with him and so closely watched him; he has been a little person of delightful, lovable goodness. You might have made the same claim for him if you had not, as it happened, seen an exception. What was your exception, and to what in your personal observation of him did you refer?"

It was a grave inquiry, but lightness was not our note, and, at any rate, before the gray dawn forced us to separate, I had got my answer. What my friend had had in mind proved to be very much to the purpose. It was neither more nor less than that, for a period of several months, Quint and the boy had been always together.

It was right that she had dared to criticize the rightness of so close an alliance, and even to go so far as to speak to Miss Jessel. Miss Jessel had, with a strange manner, requested her to mind her own business, and the good woman had, on this, approached little Miles. What she said to him, since I pressed, was that SHE liked to see young gentlemen not forget their station.

I pressed again, of course, at this.

"You reminded him that Quint was a base menial?"

"You might say! And it was his answer, for one thing, that was bad."

"And for another thing?" I waited. "He repeated your words to Quint?"

"No, not that. It's just what he WOULDN'T! I was sure, at any rate," she added, "that he didn't. But he denied certain occasions."

"What occasions?"

"When they had been about together quite as if Quint were his tutor—and a very grand one—and Miss Jessel only for the little lady.

When he had gone off with the little fellow, I mean, and spent hours with him."

"He then lied about it—he said he hadn't?" Her assent was clear enough to cause me to add. "I see. He lied."

"Oh!" Mrs. Grose mumbled. This was a suggestion that it didn't matter; which she backed up by a further remark.

"After all, Miss Jessel didn't mind. She didn't forbid him."

I considered.

"Did he put that to you as a reason?"

"No, he never spoke of it."

"Never mentioned her in connection with Quint?"

She saw, flushing, where I was coming out.

"Well, he didn't show anything. He denied," she repeated; "he denied."

Lord, how I pressed her now!

"So that you could see he knew what was between the two wretches?"

"I don't know—I don't know!" the woman groaned.

"You do know, you dear thing," I replied; "only you haven't my terrible boldness, and you keep back, out of modesty and delicacy, even in the past, when you had, without my aid, to flounder about in silence. It must have made you very unhappy. But I shall get it out of you yet! There was something in the boy that suggested to you," I continued, "that he covered and concealed their relation."

"Oh, he couldn't prevent—"

"Your learning the truth? I daresay! But, heavens," I fell to thinking, "what it shows is what they must, to that extent, have succeeded in making of him!"

"Nothing that's not nice NOW!" Mrs. Grose begged.

"I don't wonder you looked odd," I persisted, "when I mentioned to you the letter from his school!"

"I doubt if I looked as odd as you!" she answered with homely force. "And if he was so bad then, as far as that goes, how is he such an angel now?"

"Yes, if he was so bad at school! How? Well," I said in my pain, "you must put it to me again, but I shall not be able to tell you for some days. Only, put it to me again!" I cried in a way that made my friend stare. "There are directions in which I must not for the present go."

Meanwhile I returned to her first example—the one she mentioned—the boy's ability to have an occasional slip.

"If Quint—at the time you speak of—was a base menial, one of the things Miles said to you, I find myself guessing, was that you were another."

Again her admission was so adequate that I continued.

"And you forgave him that?"

"Wouldn't YOU?"

"Oh, yes!" And we exchanged there, in the stillness, a sound of the oddest amusement. Then I went on.

"At all events, while he was with the man—"

"Miss Flora was with the woman. It suited them all!"

It suited me, too, I felt, only too well; by which I mean that it suited exactly the deadly view I was in the act of forbidding myself to entertain. But I so far succeeded in checking the expression of this view that I will throw, just here, no further light on it than may be offered by the mention of my final statement to Mrs. Grose.

"His having lied and been impudent are, I confess, less engaging examples than I had hoped to have from you of the outbreak in him of the little natural man. Still," I said, "They must do, for they make me feel more than ever that I must watch."

It made me blush the next minute to see in my friend's face how much more she had forgiven him than her story struck me as presenting to me an occasion for so doing. This came out when, at the school-room door, she was about to leave.

"Surely you don't accuse HIM—" she declared.

"Of carrying on a relationship he conceals from me? Ah, remember that, until further evidence, I accuse nobody." Then, before shutting her out to go to her own place, "I must just wait," I wound up.

IX

I WAITED AND waited, and the days as they passed took something from my anxiety, most of them passing in constant sight of my pupils without a fresh incident, which was enough to brush away many of my fancies and ugly memories. The surrender to the children's grace was a thing I could easily do, and it may be imagined if I neglected to address myself to this source for whatever it would yield.

Stranger than I can express, certainly, was the effort to struggle against my new lights; it would doubtless have been, however, a greater tension still had it not been so frequently successful. I used to wonder how my little charges could help not guessing that I thought strange things about them; and the fact that these only made them more interesting was not an aid to keeping them in the dark.

I trembled lest they should see that they WERE so much more interesting. Putting things at the worst, as in thinking about it I so often did, any clouding of their innocence could only be—blameless as they were—a reason the more for taking risks. There were moments when I found myself catching them up and pressing them to my heart.

As soon as I had done so I used to say to myself, "What will they think of that? Doesn't it show too much?" It would have been easy to get into a sad, wild tangle about how much I might show; but the real account of the hours of peace I still enjoyed was that the present charm of my companions was still effective, even under the shadow of the possibility that it was studied. For it occurred to me that I might occasionally excite suspicion by the little outbreaks of my sharper passion for them. So, too, I remember wondering if I mightn't see an increase of something odd in them.

They were at this period evidently very fond of me; which, after all, I thought, was no more than a response to forever being bowed to and hugged. This fondness, of which they were so generous, succeeded, in truth, in calming my nerves quite as well as if I never appeared, to myself, as trying to catch them at a purpose in it.

They had never, I think, wanted to do so many things for their poor protector; I mean—though they got their lessons better and better, which was naturally what would please me most—in the way of entertaining or surprising me: reading passages to me, telling me stories, acting out little scenes, jumping out at me disguised as animals or historical characters—above all, astonishing me by the "pieces" they secretly got by heart. They had shown from the first a talent for everything, a general ability which made it possible for them to do remarkable things.

They went at their little tasks as if they loved them, and accomplished, from the mere out-pouring of their gift, little miracles of memory. They not only jumped out at me as tigers and Romans, but as Shakespeareans, astronomers, and navigators. This was so much the case that it had much to do with the fact as to which, at the present day, I am at a loss for a different explanation: my calmness on the subject of another school for Miles.

What I remember is that I was content not, for the time, to bring up the question, and that contentment must have sprung from the sense of his forever striking a show of cleverness. He was too clever for a bad governess, for a parson's daughter, to spoil; and the strangest, if not the brightest thread in the calmness I felt was the impression I might have got, if I had dared to work it out, that Miles was under some influence operating in his small intellectual life that was of great encouragement to him.

If it was easy to think that such a boy could put off returning to school; it was at least as marked that for such a boy to have been "kicked out" by a schoolmaster was a mystery without end. Let me add that in their company —and I was careful almost never to be out of it—I could follow no scent very far. We lived in a cloud of music and love and success and private theatricals. The musical sense in each of them was of the quickest, but the elder especially was a marvel at catching and repeating things.

The school-room piano broke into all kinds of odd fancies; and when that failed there were whispers in corners, with the sequel of one of them going out in the highest spirits in order to "come in" as something new.

I had had brothers myself, and it was not new to me that little girls could look up to little boys. But what passed everything was that there was a little boy in the world who could have for the inferior age, sex, and intelligence so fine a consideration.

They were very much at one, and to say they never quarreled or complained is to make the note of praise coarse for their quality of sweetness. Sometimes I perhaps came across traces of little understandings between them, by which one of them should keep me occupied while the other slipped away. There is a simple side, I suppose, in all diplomacy; but if my pupils practiced it upon me, it was not noticed. It was in another quarter that, after a bit, it became noticeable.

I find that I'm really hanging back now, but I must take my plunge. There came suddenly an hour after which, as I look back, the affair seems to me to have been all pure suffering; but I have at least reached the heart of it, and the straightest road out is undoubtedly to advance.

One evening—with nothing to lead up to or prepare for it—I felt the cold touch of the impression that had breathed on me the night of my arrival, and which, much lighter then, I should probably have made little of in memory had my stay there been less upsetting. I had not gone to bed; I sat reading by a couple of candles. There was a roomful of old books at Bly—last-century fiction, some of which I had never read. The book in my hand was Fielding's *Amelia*; also, I was wholly awake.

I recall both a general sense that it was very late and a particular objection to looking at my watch. I looked, finally, at the white curtain draping the head of Flora's little bed to make sure it covered the perfection of childish rest. I recollect in short that, though I was deeply interested in my author, I found myself, at the turn of a page and with his spell scattered, looking straight up and hard at the door of my room.

There was a moment during which I listened that reminded of the faint sense I had had the first night of there being something stirring in the house, and I saw the soft breath of the open window move the half-drawn blind. Then, with a deliberation that must have seemed magnificent had there been anyone to admire it, I put down my book, rose to my feet, and, taking a candle, went out of the room and, from the hall, on which my light had little effect, quietly closed and locked the door.

I can say now neither what made me do it, nor what guided me, but I went along the hall, holding my candle high, till I came within sight of the tall window at the turn of the staircase. At this point I found myself aware of three things, practically at the same time. First, my candle went out, and I saw by the uncovered window that the dusk of earliest morning made it unnecessary. The next instant I saw there was someone on the stair. I speak of sequences, but I required no lapse of seconds to stiffen myself for a third encounter with Quint.

The apparition had reached the landing halfway up and was on the spot nearest the window. At sight of me, it stopped and fixed me exactly as it had from the tower and from the garden. He knew me as well as I knew him; and so, in the cold, faint light of early dawn, with a glimmer in the high glass and another on the polish of the oak stair below, we faced each other.

He was absolutely, on this occasion, a living, hateful, dangerous presence. But that was not the wonder of wonders; I reserve this for something that was quite different: the fear had left me and there was nothing in me that didn't meet and measure him.

I had plenty of suffering after that moment, but I had, thank God, no terror. And he knew I had not—I found myself at the end of an instant very aware of this. I felt a fierce confidence that, if I stood my ground I should cease—for the time, at least—to have him to reckon with; and during that time the thing was as human and ugly as a real interview: ugly because it WAS human, as human as something to have met alone in the small hours in a sleeping house, some enemy, someone who had broken in, some criminal.

It was the dead silence of our long gaze at such close quarters that gave the whole horror, huge as it was, its only note of the unnatural. If I had met a murderer in such a place and at such an hour, we still at least would have spoken. Something would have passed between us; if nothing had passed, one of us would have moved.

The moment lasted so long that it would have taken but little more to make me doubt if even *I* were in life. I can't express what followed save by saying that the silence itself—which was in a manner proof of my strength—became the element into which I saw the figure disappear. I saw it turn as I might have seen the low wretch to which it had once belonged turn on receipt of an order, and pass, with my eyes on its evil back, down the staircase and into the darkness in the next bend.

I REMAINED A while at the top of the stair, not presently understanding that when my visitor had gone, he had gone: then I returned to my room. The first thing I saw by the light of the candle I had left burning was that Flora's bed was empty; and I caught my breath with all the terror that, five minutes before, I had been able to resist.

I dashed at the place in which I had left her lying and over which the small silk bed-spread and sheets were mixed up. The white curtains had been pulled forward; then my step, to my great relief, produced an answering sound. I saw the window blind move, and the child came from the other side of it. She stood there in her little night-gown, with her pink bare feet and the golden glow of her curls, looking very grave.

I had never had such a sense of losing an advantage as she said, "You naughty: where HAVE you been?"

Instead of challenging her. I found myself accused and explaining. She herself explained, for that matter, with the loveliest, most eager, simple manner, that she had known suddenly, as she lay there, that I was out of the room, and had jumped up to see what had become of me.

I had dropped, with the joy of her appearance, back into my chair—feeling a little faint. She came straight to me, threw herself upon my knee, and gave herself to be held, with the flame of the candle full in the wonderful little face that was still flushed with sleep.

I closed my eyes an instant, yielding before the excess of something beautiful that shone out of the blue of her eyes before speaking.

"You were looking for me out of the window?" I said. "You thought I might be walking in the grounds?"

"Well, you know, I thought someone was"—she never changed her expression as she smiled out that at me.

Oh, how I looked at her now!

"And did you see anyone?"

"NO!" she returned, with a long sweetness in her little drawl of the negative.

At that moment, in the state of my nerves, I absolutely believed she lied; and if I once more closed my eyes it was before the dazzle of the three or four possible ways in which I might take this up. One of these, for a moment, tempted me with such intensity that, to withstand it, I must have gripped my little girl with a tightness that, wonderfully, she submitted to without a cry. Why not break out at her and have it over?—give it to her straight in her lovely little face?

"You see, you see, you KNOW that you do, and that you already quite suspect I believe it; so why not confess it so that we may at least live with it together and learn perhaps, in the strangeness of our fate, where we are and what it means?"

This questioning dropped, alas, as it came: if I could have given in to it I might have spared myself—well, you'll see what. Instead of that I sprang to my feet, looked at her bed, and took a helpless middle way.

"Why did you pull the curtain over the place to make me think you were still there?"

Flora considered this, after which, with her divine smile, she said, "Because I don't like to frighten you!"

"But if I had, by your idea, gone out—?"

She absolutely declined to be puzzled; she turned her eyes to the flame of the candle as if the question were not to the point, or at any rate not personal.

"Oh, but you know," she answered, "that you might come back, you dear, and that you HAVE!"

After a little, when she had got back into bed, I had, for a long time, sitting next to her, to hold her hand to prove that I recognized the importance of my return.

You may imagine the general nature, from that moment, of my nights. I repeatedly sat up till I didn't know when; I selected moments when my room-mate was clearly asleep, and, stealing out, took noiseless turns in the hall, and even pushed as far as to where I had last met Quint. But I never met him there again; and I may as well say at once that I on no other occasion did I see him in the house. I just missed, on the staircase, on the other hand, a different adventure.

Looking down it from the top I once recognized the presence of a woman seated on one of the lower steps with her back to me, her body half-bowed and her head, in an attitude of woe, in her hands. I had been there but an instant, however, when she vanished without looking round at me. I knew, nevertheless, exactly what terrible face she had to show; and I wondered whether, if instead of being above I had been below, I should have had, for going up, the same nerve I had lately shown Quint.

Well, there continued to be plenty of chance for nerve. On the eleventh night after my encounter with that gentleman—they were all numbered now—I had an alarm that dangerously skirted it, and that, from the quality of its unexpectedness, proved quite my sharpest shock. It was precisely the first night during this series that, weary with watching, I had felt that I might again without anxiety lay myself down at my old hour.

I slept immediately and, as I afterward knew, till about one o'clock; but when I woke it was to sit straight up, as completely roused as if a hand had shaken me. I had left a light burning, but it was now out, and I felt an instant certainty that Flora had put it out. This brought me to my feet and straight, in the darkness, to her bed, which I found she had left. A glance at the window explained it further, and the striking of a match completed the picture.

The child had again got up—this time blowing out the candle, and had again, for some purpose of observing or responding, squeezed in behind the blind and was peering out into the night. That she now saw—as she had not, I had satisfied myself, the previous time—was proved by the fact that she was disturbed neither by my lighting the candle nor by the hurry I made to get to her.

Hidden, protected, completely absorbed, she rested her arms on the sill—the window opened forward—and gave herself up. There was a great still moon to help her, and this fact counted in my quick decision. She was face to face with the apparition we had met at the lake, and could now communicate with it as she had not before been able to do. What I, on my side, had to care for was, without disturbing her, to reach, from the hall, some other window in the same quarter to look out.

I got to the door without her hearing me; I got out of it, closed it, and listened from the other side for some sound from her. While I stood there I had my eyes on her brother's door, which was but ten steps off, and which produced in me again the strange impulse I lately spoke of as my temptation. What if I should go straight in and march to HIS window?—what if, by risking to his boyish bewilderment a revelation of my motive, I should throw across the rest of the mystery the reach of my boldness?

This thought held me sufficiently to make me cross to his threshold and pause again. I listened intently; I figured to myself what might possibly be; I wondered if his bed were also empty and he too were secretly at watch. It was a deep, soundless minute, at the end of which my impulse failed. He was quiet; he might be innocent; the risk was too terrible; I turned away.

There was a figure in the grounds—a figure prowling for a sight, the visitor with whom Flora was engaged; but it was not the visitor most concerned with my boy. I hesitated again, but on other grounds, and only for a few seconds; then I made my choice. There were empty rooms at Bly, and I had only to choose the right one.

The right one suddenly presented itself to me as the lower one in the corner of the house that I have spoken of as the old tower. This was a large, square chamber, arranged with some state as a bedroom, the extravagant size of which made it so inconvenient that it had not for years, though kept by Mrs. Grose in perfect order, been occupied.

I had often admired it and I knew my way about in it; I had only, after just faltering at the first chill gloom of its disuse, to pass across it and open as quietly as I could one of the blinds. Achieving this, I uncovered the glass without a sound and, applying my face to the pane, was able, the darkness without being much less than within, to see that I commanded the right direction.

Then I saw something more. The moon made the night very clear, and showed me on the lawn a person, made smaller by distance, who stood there motionless, and as if fascinated, looking up to where I had appeared—looking, that is, not so much at me as at something that was apparently above me. There was clearly another person above me—there was a person on the tower; but the presence on the lawn was not in the least what I had conceived and had hurried to meet.

The presence on the lawn was poor little Miles himself.

XI

IT WAS NOT till late next day that I spoke to Mrs. Grose; the care I took to keep my pupils in sight often made it difficult to meet her privately. In addition to this, we each felt the importance of not provoking—on the part of the servants, quite as much as on that of the children—any suspicion of a secret, or a discussion of mysteries.

I drew a great security from her smooth face. There was nothing in it to pass on to others my terrible confidences. She believed me, I was sure. If she hadn't I don't know what I would have done, for I couldn't have borne the business alone. But she was a great example of a want of imagination, and if she could see in our little charges nothing but their beauty and good nature, she had no direct contact with my trouble.

If the children had been at all marked, she would doubtless have grown, on tracing it back, haggard enough; as matters stood, however, I could feel her, when she looked at them with her large white arms folded and the habit of calmness in her face, that, if they were ruined, the pieces would still serve.

Flights of fancy gave place in her mind to a steady fireside glow, and I had already begun to see how, with the growth of the conviction that—as time went on without a public accident—our young things could, after all, look out for themselves, she addressed her greatest concern to the sad case presented by their instructor. That, for me, was a sound but simple way to look at it. I could engage that, to the world, my face should tell no tales, but it would have been an added strain to find myself anxious about hers.

At the hour I now speak of she had joined me on the terrace where, with the passing of the season, the afternoon sun was now pleasant; and we sat there together while before us, at a distance but within call if we wished, the children strolled to and fro. They moved slowly together below us, over the lawn, the boy reading aloud from a story-book and his arm round his sister to keep her quite in touch.

Mrs. Grose watched them peacefully; then I caught the intellectual stir with which she turned to take from me a view of the back of the tapestry. I had made her a receiver of many shocking things, but there was an odd recognition of my superiority—my accomplishments and function—in her patience under my anxiety. She offered her mind to my disclosures as, had I wished to mix a witch's broth and proposed she drink it, she would have held out a large clean saucepan.

This had become completely her attitude by the time that, in my telling her of the events of the night, I reached the point of what Miles had said to me when, after seeing him, at such an hour, almost on the very spot where he happened now to be. I had gone down to bring him in. Having left her meanwhile in little doubt of my small hope of representing with success, even to her, my sense of the really splendid manner in which, after I got him into the house, the boy had met my challenge.

As soon as I appeared in the moonlight on the terrace, he had come to me as straight as possible; on which I had taken his hand without a word and led him, through the dark spaces, up the staircase where Quint had so hungrily waited for him, along the hall where I had listened and trembled, and so to his room.

Not a sound, on the way, passed between us, and I wondered— oh, HOW I had wondered!—if he were groping about in his little mind for something that was not too strange to say to me. It would tax his invention, and I felt, this time, over his real embarrassment, a curious thrill of victory. It was a sharp trap for the boy! He couldn't play any longer at not knowing; so how would he get out of it? There beat in me, with the passion of this question, an equal appeal as to how *I* should.

I was met at last, as never yet, with all the risk attached to sounding my own terrible note. I remember that, as we pushed into his little room where the bed had not been slept in, the window, uncovered to the moonlight, made the place so clear that there was no need of striking a match—I remember how I suddenly sank upon the edge of the bed from the force of the idea that he must know how he really, as they say, "had" me.

He could do what he liked, with all his cleverness, so long as I should continue to believe those care-takers of the young who minister to their fears are criminals. He "had" me indeed; for who would ever forgive me, who would consent that I should go free, if, by the faintest mention, I were the first to introduce into our perfect relationship an element so evil?

No, it was useless to attempt to say this to Mrs. Grose, just as it is scarcely less so to attempt to suggest here, how, in our short brush in the dark, he shook me with the thought of how admirable he was. I was of course most kind and merciful; never yet had I placed on his shoulders hands of such tenderness as those with which I held him there. I had no choice but to put it to him.

"You must tell me now—and all the truth. What did you go out for? What were you doing there?"

I can still see his wonderful smile, the whites of his beautiful eyes, and his little teeth shining in the dusk.

"If I tell you why, will you understand?"

My heart at this leaped into my mouth. WOULD he tell me? I replied only with a nod. He was gentleness itself, and while he lay there he was more than ever a little prince. It was his brightness that put me at ease. Was he really going to tell me?

"Well," he said at last, "just exactly in order that you should do this."

"Do what?"

"Think me—for a change—BAD!"

I shall never forget the sweetness with which he said this, nor how, on top of it, he bent forward and kissed me. It was practically the end of everything. I met his kiss and I had to make, while I folded him for a minute in my arms, the greatest effort not to cry. He had given exactly the account of himself that permitted least of my going behind it, and it was only with the effect of my acceptance of it that, as I glanced about the room, I said:

"Then you didn't undress at all?"

He fairly glittered in the gloom.

"Not at all. I sat up and read."

"And when did you go down?"

"At midnight. When I'm bad I AM bad!"

"I see, I see—it's charming. But how could you be sure I would know it?"

"Oh, I arranged that with Flora." His answers rang out with readiness! "She was to get up and look out."

"Which is what she did do."

It was I who fell into the trap!

"So she disturbed you, and, to see what she was looking at, you also looked out—you saw."

"While you," I said, "caught your death in the night air!"

He literally bloomed from this trick.

"How otherwise should I have been bad enough?" he asked. Then, after another embrace, the incident closed on my recognizing all the reserves of goodness that, for his joke, he had been able to draw upon.

XII

THE IMPRESSION I received proved, in the morning light, not quite something I could present to Mrs. Grose, though I backed it up with the mention of still another remark that Miles had made before we separated.

"It all lies in five short words," I said to her, "words that really settle the matter: 'Think what I MIGHT do!' He threw that off to show me how good he is. He knows down to the ground what he 'might' do. That's what he gave them a taste of at school."

"Lord, you do change!" cried my friend.

"I don't change—I simply make it out. The four, depend upon it, are always meeting. If on any of these last nights you had been with either child, you would understand. The more I've watched and waited, the more I've felt that, if there were nothing else to make it certain, it would be made so by the silence of each. NEVER, by a slip of the tongue, have they so much as mentioned their old friends, any more than Miles has said anything about his expulsion. Oh, yes, we may sit here and watch them show off to us to their fill; but even while they pretend to be lost in their fairy-tale, they're deep in their vision of the dead brought back to life. He's not reading to her," I declared; "they're talking of THEM—they're talking of evil! I go on, I know, as if I were crazy; it's a wonder I'm not. What I've seen would have made YOU so; but it has only made me clearer."

My being so clear must have seemed awful to her, but the charming creatures who were the victims of it, passing back and forth in their sweetness, gave her something to hold on by; and I felt how tight she held as, without being stirred by my passion, she looked at them.

"What other things are you clearer about?"

"Why, the very things that have delighted, fascinated, and yet, at bottom, as I now see, mystified and troubled me: Their more than earthly beauty, their more than natural goodness. It's a game," I went on; "it's false!"

"On the part of little darlings—?"

"As yet mere lovely babies? Yes, mad as that seems!"

The act of bringing it out helped me piece it together.

"They haven't been good—they've only been absent. It has been easy to live with them because they're simply leading a life of their own. They're not mine—they're not ours. They're *his* and *hers*!"

"Quint's and that woman's?"

"Quint's and that woman's. They want to get to them."

How, at this, poor Mrs. Grose appeared to study them!

"But for what?"

"For the love of the evil that, in those days, the pair put into them. To supply them with that evil still, to keep up the work of the devil, is what brings them back."

"Laws!" said my friend under her breath.

The expression was plain, but it showed an acceptance of my further proof of what, in the bad time—for there had been a worse time even than this!—must have occurred. There could have been no greater proof for me than the agreement of her experience to whatever depth of evil I found one could believe in our scoundrels.

"They WERE rascals! But what can they now do?"

"Do?" I echoed it so loud that Miles and Flora, as they passed at their distance, paused in their walk and looked at us. "Don't they do enough?" I demanded in a lower tone, while the children, having smiled and nodded and kissed hands to us, went on with their display.

We were held by it a minute; then I answered, "They can destroy them!"

At this my companion turned, but her inquiry was a silent one, the effect of which was to make me go on.

"They don't know as yet quite how—but they're trying. They're seen only across and beyond, as it were—in strange places and high places, the top of towers, the roof of houses, outside of windows, the further edge of pools; but there's a deep design on either side to shorten that distance and overcome the divide; and their success is only a question of time."

"For the children to come?"

"And perish in the attempt!"

Mrs. Grose slowly got up, and I added, "Unless, of course, we can prevent it!"

Standing before me, she turned things over, and then said, "Their uncle must prevent it. He must take them away."

"And who's to make him?"

She had been looking into the distance, but she now dropped on me a foolish face.

"You, miss."

"By writing to him that his house is poisoned and his little nephew and niece mad?"

"But if they ARE, miss?"

"And if I am myself, you mean? That's charming news to be sent by a governess whose main task was supposed to be to give him no worry."

Mrs. Grose considered, following the children again.

"Yes, he do hate worry. That was the great reason—"

"Why those evil friends took him in so long? Well, at any rate, I'm not evil; I shouldn't take him in."

My companion sat down and grasped my arm.

"Make him at any rate come to you."

I stared.

"To ME?"

I had a sudden fear of what she might do.

"He ought to BE here—he ought to help,"

I rose, and I must have shown an odder face than ever.

"You see me asking him for a visit?"

No, with her eyes on my face she evidently couldn't. Instead, she saw what I saw: his scorn, his amusement, his contempt for the breakdown of my acceptance at being left alone, and for the fine machinery I had set in motion to attract his attention to my slighted charms.

She didn't know—no one knew—how proud I had been to serve him, and stick to our terms; yet she took the measure, I think, of the warning I now gave her.

"If you should lose your head and appeal to him—"

She was really frightened.

"Yes, miss?"

"I would leave, on the spot, both him and you."

XIII

THIS SITUATION CONTINUED a month, and with new notes, the note above all, sharper and sharper, of the "knowing" of the evil on the part of my pupils. It was not, I'm as sure today as I was then, just my imagination: it was absolutely certain they knew of my problem, and that this made, for a long time, the air in which we moved.

I don't mean they had their tongues in their cheeks or did anything common, for that was not one of their dangers. I mean that the element of the unnamed and untouched became, between us, greater than any other, and that our avoiding it could not have been so successful without much quiet arranging of things.

It was as if, at moments, we were forever coming into sight of subjects before which we must stop short, turning suddenly out of alleys that we saw to be blind, and closing with a little bang that made us look at each other—for, like all bangs, it was louder than we had intended—the doors we had opened.

There were times when it might have struck us that almost every branch of study or subject of conversation skirted forbidden ground. Forbidden ground was the question of the return of the dead in general, and of whatever might survive in their memory of the friends the children had lost. There were days when I could have sworn that one of them had, with a small unseen nudge, said to the other:

"She thinks she'll do it this time—but she WON'T!"

To "do it" would have been to indulge in some direct reference to the lady who had prepared them for my instruction. They had a delightful, endless appetite for stories in my own history, to which

I again and again treated them. They knew just about everything that had ever happened to me; they had had the story of my smallest adventures, and of those of my brothers and sisters, as well as particulars about the odd nature of my father, and even how our furniture was arranged.

There were things enough to chatter about, if one went very fast and knew by instinct when to go round. They pulled with an art of their own the strings of my invention and memory; and nothing else perhaps, when I thought of it afterward, gave me so the suspicion of being watched from under cover.

It was in any case over MY life, MY past, and MY friends alone that we could take anything like our ease—a state of affairs that led them, sometimes, to break out into sociable reminders of my past. I was invited to repeat again Goody Gosling's celebrated *mot* or to confirm details as to the cleverness of our small horse.

It was partly at such times as these that, with the turn matters had now taken, my problem, as I called it, grew most real to me. The fact that the days passed without another encounter ought, it would have appeared, to have done something toward soothing my nerves, but it didn't.

Since the light brush that second night on the upper landing with the presence of a woman at the foot of the stair, I had seen nothing, in or out of the house, that one had better not have seen. There was many a corner round which I expected to come upon Quint, and many a situation that, in a sinister way, would have favored the appearance of Miss Jessel.

The summer had gone; the autumn was upon Bly and the place, with its gray sky and dried gardens, its bared spaces and scattered leaves, was like a theater after the performance—strewn with crumpled playbills. There was something in the air, of sound and stillness, impressions that brought back to me the feeling in which, that June evening out of doors, I had had my first sight of Quint, and the other instant when, after seeing him through the window, I had looked for him in the circle of bushes.

I recognized the signs, the moment, the spot. But they remained empty, and I continued free of *them*, if that's what one could call a young woman whose sensibility had, in the oddest fashion, not declined but deepened. I had said in my talk with Mrs. Grose on that terrible scene with Flora's by the lake—and had puzzled her by saying it—that it would from that moment worry me more to lose my power than to keep it. I had expressed what was so clearly in my mind: the truth that, whether the children really saw or not—since it was not yet definitely proved—I greatly preferred, as a safeguard, my own exposure. I was ready to know the worst.

What I feared was that my eyes might be sealed just as theirs were opened. Well, my eyes WERE sealed, it appeared, at present—for which it seemed a sin not to thank God. There was, alas, a difficulty about that: I would have thanked him with all my soul had I not had in equal measure this sure belief in the secret of my pupils.

How can I trace today the strange steps of my concern? There were times of our being together when I would have been ready to swear that, in my presence but with my direct sense of it closed, they had visitors who were known and welcome. Then it was that, had I not been held back by the chance that such an injury might prove greater than the injury to be avoided, my sense of victory would have broken out.

"They're here, they're here, you little wretches," I would have cried, "and you can't deny it now!"

The little wretches denied it with all the added volume of their sociability and their tenderness, in the crystal depths of which—like the flash of a fish in a stream—the mockery of their advantage peeped up. The shock, in truth, had sunk into me still deeper than I knew on the night when, looking out to see either Quint or Miss Jessel, I had seen the boy, over whose rest I watched, turn on me the lovely upward look with which, from the battlements above, the apparition of Quint had appeared.

If it was a question of a scare, my discovery on this occasion had scared me more than any other, and it was in the condition of nerves produced by it that I concluded what I did. They troubled me so that sometimes, at odd moments, I shut myself up to rehearse out loud—it was at once a relief and a renewed despair—the manner in which I might come to the point.

I approached it from one side and the other while, in my room, I flung myself about, but I always broke down in speaking their names. As they died away on my lips, I said to myself that if I should indeed help them to talk about something evil by pronouncing their names, I should violate as rare a case of the need to be delicate as any schoolroom, probably, had ever known.

When I said to myself, "THEY have the manners to be silent, and you, trusted as you are, have the baseness to speak!" I felt myself redden, and I covered my face.

After these secret scenes I talked more than ever, loudly enough, till one of our long silences occurred—the strange, dizzy lift into a stillness, a pause of all life, that had nothing to do with the noise that at the moment we might be making. Then it was that the others, the outsiders, were there. They caused me, while they stayed, to tremble with fear of their addressing to their younger victims some yet more evil message or more vivid image than they had thought good enough for me.

What it was almost impossible to get rid of was the cruel idea that, whatever I had seen, Miles and Flora saw MORE—things so terrible I couldn't even guess, that sprang from dreadful scenes in the past. Such things naturally left, for the time, a chill which we loudly denied we felt; and we had, all three of us, with repetition, got into such splendid training that we went, each time, almost automatically, to mark the close of the incident, through the very same movements.

It was striking of the children, at all events, to kiss me and never to fail—one or the other—of asking the precious question that had helped us through many a dangerous moment: "When do you think he WILL come? Don't you think we OUGHT to write?"

There was nothing like that inquiry, we found by experience, for carrying off our lack of ease.

"He" of course was their uncle in Harley Street; and we lived much in this theory that he might at any moment arrive. It was impossible to give less encouragement than he had done to such a doctrine, but if we had not had the doctrine to fall back upon we should have deprived each other of some of our finest moments.

He never wrote to them—that may have been selfish, but it was a part of his trust of me; for the way in which a man pays his highest tribute to a woman is apt to be but by the sacred law of his comfort; and I held that I carried out the spirit of the pledge given not to appeal to him when I let my charges understand that their own letters were to be but charming literary exercises.

They were too beautiful to be posted; I kept them myself, and have them all to this hour. This was a rule which only added to the effect of my being plied with the idea that he might at any moment be among us. It was exactly as if my charges knew how almost more awkward than anything else that might be for me.

There appears to me, moreover, as I look back, no note in all this more extra-ordinary than the fact that, in spite of my tension and of their triumph, I never lost patience with them. Adorable they must in truth have been, I now reflect, that I didn't in these days hate them!

Would my anxiety, however, if relief had longer been postponed, finally have betrayed me? It little matters, for relief arrived. I call it relief, though it was only the relief that a snap brings to a strain, or a thunderstorm to a day of heat. It was at least change, and it came with a rush.

XIV

WALKING TO CHURCH one Sunday morning, I had little Miles at my side and his sister, in advance of us, at Mrs. Grose's side. It was a crisp, clear day; the night had brought a touch of frost, and the autumn air, bright and sharp, made the church bells almost gay.

I happened at such a moment to be very gratefully struck with the obedience of my little charges. Why did they never resent my ever-present-society? Something brought nearer the idea that I had all but pinned the boy to my shawl. I was like a jailer with an eye to possible escapes. All this belonged—their total surrender—to facts that were most terrible.

Decked out for Sunday by his uncle's tailor, who had had a free hand and a notion of pretty waist-coats, with his grand air, Miles's title to independence, the rights of his sex and situation, were so stamped upon him that if he had suddenly struck for freedom I should have had nothing to say. I was by chance wondering how I should meet him, when the revolution occurred.

"Look here, my dear," he charmingly said, "when in the world, please, am I going back to school?"

Seen here, the speech sounds harmless enough, especially as uttered in the sweet, high, casual voice with which he threw off words as if he were tossing roses. There was something in them that always made one "catch," and I caught it now so effectually that I stopped short, as if a tree had fallen across the road.

This was something new between us, and he was perfectly aware that I recognized it, though, to enable me to do so, he had no need to look a bit less open and charming than usual. I could feel in him how he already, at my first finding nothing to reply, saw the advantage he had gained. I was so slow to find anything to say that he had plenty of time to continue, with a suggestive smile:

"You know, my dear, for a fellow to be with a lady ALWAYS—!" His "my dear" was constantly on his lips and nothing could have expressed more the exact shade of the sentiment I desired to inspire in my pupils than its fond familiarity. It was so respectfully easy.

But, oh, how I felt that at present I must pick my own phrases! I remember that, to gain time, I tried to laugh, and I seemed to see in the beautiful face with which he watched me how ugly and odd I looked.

"And always with the same lady?" I returned.

He didn't pause, and it was out between us.

"Ah, of course, she's a jolly, 'perfect' lady; but, after all, I'm a fellow, don't you see, that's—well, getting on."

I lingered there with him an instant ever so kindly.

"Yes, you're getting on."

I felt helpless! I have kept to this day the heartbreaking idea of how he seemed to know that and to play with it.

"You can't say I've not been good, can you?"

I laid my hand on his shoulder, for, though I felt it would be better to walk on, I was not quite able to do so.

"No, I can't say that, Miles."

"Except just that one night, you know—!"

"That one night?"

I couldn't look as straight as he.

"Why, when I went down—went out of the house."

"Oh, yes. But I forget what you did it for."

"You forget?"—he spoke with sweet childish reproach. "Why, it was to show you I could!"

"Oh, yes, you could."

"And I can again."

I felt that I might, perhaps, after all, succeed in keeping my wits about me.

"Certainly. But you won't."

"No, not THAT again. It was nothing."

"It was nothing," I said. "But we must go on."

We resumed walking as he put his hand into my arm.

"Then when AM I going back?"

I wore, in turning it over, my most responsible air.

"Were you very happy at school?"

He just considered.

"Oh, I'm happy enough anywhere!"

"Well, then," I said, "if you're just as happy here—!"

"But it isn't everything! Of course, YOU know a lot—"

"But you hint that you know almost as much?" I risked.

"Not half as much as I want to!" Miles answered. "But it isn't so much that."

"What is it, then?"

"Well—I want to see more life."

"I see; I see."

We had arrived in sight of the church, where various persons were on their way in or clustered about the door. I quickened our step, wanting to get there before the question between us opened up much further. For more than an hour, in church, he would have to be silent; and I thought of the dusk of the pew and the stool on which I might bend my knees. I seemed to be running a race with some confusion to which he was about to reduce me.

I felt he had got in first when, before we even entered the churchyard, he threw out, "I want my own sort!"

It made me bound forward.

"There are not many of your own sort, Miles!" I laughed. "Unless, perhaps, dear little Flora!"

"You really compare me to a baby girl?"

This found me quite weak.

"Don't you LOVE our sweet Flora?"

"If I didn't—and you, too; if I didn't—!" he repeated as if retreating for a jump, yet leaving his thought so unfinished that, after we had come into the gate, another stop, which he imposed on me, had become necessary.

Mrs. Grose and Flora had passed into the church, the other worshippers had followed, and we were for the minute alone among the old graves. We had paused on the path from the gate by a low, oblong, table-like tomb.

"Yes, if you didn't—?"

He looked, while I waited, at the grave.

"Well, you know what!" But he didn't move, and he presently produced something that made me sit on the stone slab as if suddenly to rest.

"Does my uncle think what YOU think?"

"How do you know what I think?"

"Ah, well, of course I don't; for it strikes me you never tell me. But I mean does HE know?"

"Know what, Miles?"

"Why, the way I'm going on."

I saw quickly enough that I could make no answer that would not involve a sacrifice of my employer. Yet it appeared to me that we were all, at Bly, sufficiently sacrificed to make that a minor sin.

"I don't think your uncle much cares."

Miles, on this, stood looking at me.

"Then don't you think he can be made to?"

"In what way?"

"Why, by his coming down."

"But who'll get him to come down?"

"*I* will!" the boy said with great brightness and emphasis. He gave me another look charged with that expression, and then marched off alone into church.

THE BUSINESS WAS practically settled from the moment I failed to follow him. It was a pitiful surrender, but my being aware of this had somehow no power to restore me. I sat there on my tomb and read into what he had said to me the fullness of its meaning; by the time I had grasped the whole of it I had also embraced the excuse that I was ashamed to offer my pupils such an example of delay.

What I said to myself above all was that Miles had got something out of me and that the proof of it, for him, would be just this awkward collapse. He had got out of me that there was something I was afraid of, and that he should probably be able to make use of it to gain more freedom. My fear was of having to deal with the question of his dismissal from school, for that was really the question of the terrors that had gathered behind us.

That his uncle should arrive to treat with me of these things was a solution that, strictly speaking, I ought now to have desired, but I could so little face the ugliness and pain of it that I simply put it off from day to day. The boy, to my deep discomfort, was in the right, and was in a position to say to me: "Either you clear up with my guardian the mystery of this interruption of my studies, or you cease to expect me to lead with you a life that's so unnatural for a boy."

What was so unnatural for this particular boy was his suddenly revealing that he knew of the problem and had a plan for solving it. That was what really did me in and prevented my going into the church after him. I walked around, hesitating, considering that I had already, with him, hurt myself beyond repair. Therefore I could patch up nothing, and it was too extreme an effort to squeeze beside him into the pew: he would be so much surer than ever to pass his arm into mine and make me sit there for an hour in close, silent contact with him.

For the first time since his arrival I wanted to get away from him. As I paused beneath the high east window and listened to the sounds of worship, I was taken with an impulse that I felt might master me completely, and that I should not give way to. Of course, I might easily put an end to my problem by getting away altogether.

Here was my chance; there was no one to stop me; I could give the whole thing up—turn my back and retreat. It was only a question of hurrying, for a few preparations, to the house, which the attendance at church of so many of the servants would practically have left unoccupied. No one, in short, could blame me if I should just drive off. What was it to get away if I got away only till dinner? That would be in a couple of hours, at the end of which my little pupils would play at innocent wonder about my not following in their train.

"What DID you do, you naughty, bad thing? Why in the world, to worry us so—and take our thoughts off, too, don't you know—did you desert us at the very door?"

I couldn't meet such questions nor, as they asked them, their false little lovely eyes; yet it was all so exactly what I should have to meet that, as the prospect grew sharp, I at last let myself go. I got, so far as the present moment was concerned, away; I went straight out of the church-yard and back through the park the way I had come.

It seemed to me that by the time I reached the house I had made up my mind to fly. The Sunday stillness, both of the approaches to the house and of the interior, in which I met no one, excited me with a sense of opportunity. Were I to get off quickly, I should get off without a scene. My quickness would have to be great, however, and the question of means was the big one.

Tormented in the hall with difficulties and obstacles, I remember sinking down at the foot of the stairs—collapsing on the lowest step, and then, with disgust, remembering that it was exactly there, more than a month before, in the darkness of night and just so bowed with evil things, I had seen the most terrible of women.

At this I was able to straighten myself; I went the rest of the way up the stairs and made for the school-room, where there were objects belonging to me I should have to take. But I opened the door to find, in a flash, my eyes unsealed. In the presence of what I saw I fell back on my desire to fight rather than flee.

Seated at my table in clear noonday light I saw a person whom, without my previous experience, I should have taken at first for some house-maid who might have stayed home to look after the place and who, availing herself of rare relief from observation, was using the school-room and my pens, ink, and paper to write a letter to her sweet-heart.

There was an effort in the way that, while her arms rested on the table, her hands, with evident weariness, supported her head; but at the moment I took this in I had already become aware that, in spite of my entrance, her attitude didn't change. Then it was—with the very act of its announcing itself—that her identity flared up in a change of posture.

She rose, not as if she had heard me, but with a grand air of indifference and, within a dozen feet of me, stood there as the evil woman who had had my job before me. Dishonored and tragic, she was all before me; but even as I fixed it in my memory the image passed away. Dark as midnight in her black dress, her haggard beauty and her deep sadness, she had looked at me long enough to appear to say that her right to sit at my table was as good as mine. While these instants lasted, I had the chill of feeling that it was I who didn't belong.

It was as a wild protest against it that I spoke to her, crying out, "You terrible, terrible woman!"

I heard myself break into a sound that, by way of the open door, rang through the long hall and empty house. She looked at me as if she heard me, but I had cleared the air. There was nothing in the room the next minute but the sunshine and a sense that I must stay.

XVI

I HAD SO expected that the return of my pupils would be marked by a display of some kind, that I was up-set that they said nothing about my absence. Instead of calling me out and acting loving, they made no mention of my having failed them, and I was left, on seeing that she too said nothing, to study Mrs. Grose's face.

I was sure they had in some way bribed her to silence, a silence I would try to break down on the first private opportunity. This opportunity came before tea: I secured five minutes with her in the housekeeper's room, where, in the twilight, amid a smell of freshly baked bread, I found her sitting peacefully before the fire in the dusky, shining room, everything put away.

"Oh, yes," she said, "they asked me to say nothing; and to please them—so long as they were there—I promised. But what happened to you?"

"I only went with you for the walk," I said. "I had then to come back to meet a friend."

She showed her surprise.

"A friend—YOU?"

"Oh, yes, I have a couple!" I laughed. "But did the children give you a reason?"

"For not saying anything about your leaving us? Yes; they said you would like it better. Do you like it better?"

My face had made her sad.

"No, I like it worse!" But after an instant I added, "Did they say why I should like it better?"

"No; Master Miles only said, 'We must do nothing but what she likes!'"

"I wish indeed he would. And what did Flora say?"

"Miss Flora was too sweet. She said, 'Oh, of course, of course!'—and I said the same."

I thought a moment.

"You were too sweet, too—I can hear you all. But nevertheless, between Miles and me, it's now all out."

"All out?" My companion stared. "But what, miss?"

"Everything. It doesn't matter. I've made up my mind. I came home, my dear, for a talk with Miss Jessel."

I had by this time formed the habit of having Mrs. Grose well in hand in advance of sounding that note, so that even now, as she bravely blinked under the signal of my word, I could keep her reasonably firm.

"A talk! Do you mean she spoke?"

"It came to that. I found her on my return in the school-room."

"And what did she say?"

I can hear the good woman still, and see her lack of understanding.

"That she suffers the torments—!"

It was this, of a truth, that made her mouth drop open. "Do you mean," she went on, "—of the lost?"

"Of the lost. Of the damned. And that's why, to share them—" I paused myself before the terror of it.

But my companion, with less imagination, kept me up.

"To share them—?"

"She wants Flora." Mrs. Grose might, as I gave it to her, have fallen away from me had I not been prepared. I held her. "As I've told you, however, it doesn't matter."

"Because you've made up your mind? But to what?"

"To everything."

"And what do you call 'everything'?"

"Why, sending for their uncle."

"Oh, miss, in pity do," my friend broke out.

"I will, I WILL! It's the only way. What's 'out,' as I told you, with Miles, is that if he thinks I'm afraid to—and has ideas of what he gains by that—he shall see he's mistaken. Yes, his uncle shall have it from me. If I'm to be blamed with having done nothing about his school—"

"Yes, miss—" my companion pressed me.

"Well, there's that awful reason."

There were now clearly so many of these for poor Mrs. Grose, that she was excusable for her not understanding.

"But—a—which?"

"Why, the letter from his old place."

"You'll show it to the master?"

"I ought to have done so on the instant."

"Oh, no!" said Mrs. Grose with decision.

"I'll put it before him," I went on, "that I can't undertake to work with a child who has been expelled—"

"We've never known for what!" Mrs. Grose declared.

"For wickedness. For what else—when he's so clever and beautiful and perfect? Is he stupid? Is he untidy? Is he infirm? Is he ill-natured? He's exquisite—so it can be only THAT; and that will open up the whole thing. After all," I said, "it's their uncle's fault. For he left them here with such people—!"

"He didn't really in the least know them. The fault's mine."

She had turned quite pale.

"Well, you shan't suffer," I answered.

"The children shan't!" she returned.

I was silent a while; we looked at each other.

"Then what am I to tell him?" I asked.

"You needn't tell him anything. *I'll* tell him."

I measured this.

"Do you mean you'll write—?"

But remembering she couldn't, I caught myself up.

"How do you communicate?"

"I tell the bailiff. HE writes."

"And should you like him to write our story?"

My question had a force I had not fully intended, and it made her break down. The tears were again in her eyes.

"Ah, miss, YOU write!"

"Well—tonight," I answered; and on this we separated.

XVII

I WENT so far, in the evening, as to make a beginning. The weather had changed back, a great wind was abroad, and beneath the lamp in my room, with Flora at peace beside me, I sat for a long time before a blank sheet of paper and listened to the rain and the wind.

Finally I went out, taking a candle; I crossed the hall and listened a minute at Miles's door. What I listened for was some betrayal of his not being at rest, and I presently caught one, but not in the form I had expected.

His voice rang out, "I say, you there—come in."

It was a gayness in the gloom!

I went in with my light and found him in bed, very wide awake, but very much at his ease.

"Well, what are YOU up to?" he asked with a cheerfulness in which, it occurred to me, Mrs. Grose might have looked in vain for anything that was "out."

I stood over him with my candle.

"How did you know I was there?"

"Why, I heard you. Did you fancy you made no noise? You're like a troop of horses!" he laughed.

"Then you weren't asleep?"

"Not much! I lie awake and think."

I put my candle, on purpose, a short way off, and then, as he held out his hand to me, I sat on the edge of his bed.

"What is it," I asked, "that you think of?"

"What in the world, my dear, but YOU?"

"Ah, the pride I take in your appreciation doesn't insist on that! I had so far rather you slept."

"Well, I think also, you know, of this queer business of ours."

I marked the coolness of his firm little hand.

"Of what queer business, Miles?"

"Why, the way you bring me up. And all the rest!"

I fairly held my breath, and even from my pale candle there was light enough to show how he smiled up at me.

"What do you mean by all the rest?"

"Oh, you know, you know!"

I could say nothing for a minute, though I felt, as I held his hand and our eyes continued to meet, that my silence had the air of admitting his charge, and that nothing in the whole world of reality was perhaps at that moment so strange as our actual relation.

"Certainly you shall go back to school," I said, "if it be that that troubles you. But not to the old place—we must find another, a better. How could I know it troubled you when you never told me so, never spoke of it at all?"

His face, framed in its smooth whiteness, made him for the minute as appealing as a patient in a children's hospital; and I would have given, as the resemblance came to me, all I possessed to be the nurse or sister of charity who might have helped to cure him.

"Do you know you've never said a word to me about your school—I mean the old one; never mentioned it?"

He seemed to wonder, smiling with the same loveliness. But he clearly gained time.

"Haven't I?"

It wasn't for ME to help him—it was for what I had met! Yet something in his tone and the expression of his face set my heart aching with such a pang, so touching was it to see his little brain puzzled and his resources taxed to play, under the spell laid on him, being both innocent and consistent.

"No, never—from the hour you came back. You've never mentioned to me one of your masters, one of your friends, nor the least little thing that ever happened to you. Never, little Miles—never—have you given me the least idea of anything that MAY have happened there. You can fancy how much I'm in the dark. Until you came out that way, this morning, you had, since the first hour I saw you, scarce mentioned anything in your previous life. You seemed so perfectly to accept the present."

It was beyond imaging how my absolute conviction of his being so advanced for his age (or whatever I might call the poison of an influence that I dared but half to phrase) made him, in spite of the faint breath of his inward trouble, appear as grown up as an older person—made him almost an intellectual equal.

"I thought you wanted to go on as you are," I said.

It struck me that at this he faintly colored. He gave, at any rate, like someone slightly tired, a shake of his head.

"I don't—I don't. I want to get away."

"You're tired of Bly?"

"Oh, no, I like Bly."

"Well, then—?"

"Oh, YOU know what a boy wants!"

I felt I didn't know so well as Miles.

"You want to go to your uncle?"

Again, with his sweet face, he made a movement.

"Ah, you can't get off with that!"

It was I now, I think, who changed color.

"My dear, I don't want to get off!"

"You can't, even if you do. You can't, you can't!"—he lay beautifully staring. "My uncle must come down, and you must completely settle things."

"If we do," I returned with some spirit, "you may be sure it will be to take you quite away."

"Well, don't you understand, that's exactly what I'm working for? You'll have to tell him—about the way you've let it all drop: you'll have to tell him a lot!"

The joy with which he said this helped me somehow, for the instant, to meet him rather more.

"And how much will YOU, Miles, have to tell him? There are things he'll ask you!"

He turned it over.

"Very likely. But what things?"

"The things you've never told me. To make up his mind what to do with you. He can't send you back—"

"Oh, I don't want to go back!" he broke in. "I want a new field."

He said this with admirable serenity and cheerfulness; and doubtless it was that very note that made me most sad, the childish tragedy, of his probable reappearance at the end of three months with all this brave front and still more dishonor. I should never be able to bear that, and it made me let myself go. I threw myself upon him and in the tenderness of my pity I embraced him.

"Dear little Miles, dear little Miles—!"

My face was close to his, and he let me kiss him, simply taking it with good humor.

"Well, old lady?"

"Is there nothing—nothing at all you want to tell me?"

He turned off a little, facing round toward the wall, and held up his hand to look at as a sick child might do.

"I've told you—I told you this morning."

Oh, I was sorry for him!

"That you just want me not to worry you?"

He looked at me, as if recognizing my understanding; then ever so gently said, "To let me alone."

There was an odd dignity in it, something that made me release him, yet, when I had slowly risen, linger beside him. God knows I never wished to worry him, but I felt that merely to turn my back on him was to abandon or, to put it more truly, to lose him.

"I've just begun a letter to your uncle," I said.

"Well, then, finish it!"

I waited a minute.

"What happened before?"

He gazed up at me again.

"Before what?"

"Before you came back. And before you went away."

For a time he was silent, but he still met my eyes.

"What happened?"

It made me, the sound of the words, in which it seemed to me I caught for the first time a small faint note of consent—it made me drop on my knees beside the bed and seize once more the chance of possessing him.

"Dear little Miles, if you KNEW how I want to help you! It's only that, it's nothing but that. I'd rather die than give you any pain or do you a wrong—I'd rather die than hurt a hair of you. Dear little Miles"—oh, I brought it out now even if I SHOULD go too far—"I just want you to help me to save you!"

I knew in a moment I had gone too far.

The answer to my appeal was immediate; it came in the form of a strong blast and chill, a gust of frozen air, and a shake of the room as great as if, in the wild wind, the window had crashed in. The boy gave a loud, high shriek, which, lost in the rest of the shock of sound, might have seemed, though I was so close to him, a note either of joy or of terror. I jumped to my feet, conscious of darkness.

So for a moment we remained, while I stared about and saw that the curtains were not moving and the window was tight.

"Why, the candle's out!" I cried.

"It was I who blew it, dear!" said Miles.

XVIII

THE NEXT DAY, after lessons, Mrs. Grose found a moment to say to me quietly: "Have you written, miss?"

"Yes—I've written."

But I didn't add that my letter was still in my pocket. There would be time enough to send it before the messenger should go to the village. Meanwhile there had been, on the part of my pupils, no more brilliant, more perfect morning. It was exactly as if they both wanted to smooth over any recent little friction. They performed the greatest feats of arithmetic, soaring quite out of MY feeble range, and made, in higher spirits than ever, geographical and historical jokes.

It was evidenced in Miles in particular that he appeared to wish to show how easily he could let me down. This child, to my memory, really lives in a setting of beauty and happiness that no words can describe; there was a distinction all his own in everything he did; never was a small creature a more clever, finer little gentleman.

I had forever to guard against the wonder into which my view of him led me; to check the gaze and sigh in which I constantly attacked the puzzle of what such a little gentleman could have done that deserved a penalty. I knew the imagination of all evil HAD been opened to him, but all the justice within me ached for proof that it could ever have flowered into an act.

He had never, at any rate, been such a little gentleman as when, after our early dinner on this terrible day, he came round to me and asked if I shouldn't like him, for half an hour, to play to me. It was a charming example of how pleasing he could be, and quite the same as his saying outright:

"The true knights we love to read about never push an advantage too far. I know what you mean now: you mean that—to be let alone yourself and not followed up—you'll cease to worry and spy upon me, won't keep me so close to you, will let me go and come. Well, I 'come,' you see—but I don't go! There'll be plenty of time for that. I do really delight in your society, and I only want to show you that the way I acted was for a principle."

It may be imagined whether I fought against this appeal and failed to go with him again, hand in hand, to the school-room. He sat down at the old piano and played as he had never played; and if there are those who think he had better have been kicking a football I can only say that I wholly agree with them. For at the end of a time under his influence that I quite ceased to measure, I started up with a strange sense of having slept at my post.

It was after lunch, and yet I hadn't really, in the least, slept: I had only done something much worse—I had forgotten. Where, all this time, was Flora? When I put the question to Miles, he played on a minute before answering, and then only said, "Why, my dear, how do *I* know?"—breaking moreover into a happy laugh, after which he stretched out into a crazy, gay song.

I went straight to my room, but his sister was not there; then, before going downstairs, I looked into several others. As she was nowhere about, she would surely be with Mrs. Grose, whom, in the comfort of that theory, I went in search of. I found her where I had found her the evening before, but she met my quick challenge with blank, scared ignorance. She had supposed that, after the meal, I had carried off both the children; as to which she was quite in her right, for it was the first time I had allowed the little girl out of my sight without arranging for some special care.

Of course, she might be with the maids, so that the immediate thing was to look for her without an air of alarm. This we promptly arranged between us; but when, ten minutes later, we met in the hall, it was only to report on either side that, after guarded inquiries, we had quite failed to trace her. For a minute we exchanged silent alarms, and I could feel with what high interest my friend returned me all those I had first given her.

"She'll be above," she presently said—"in one of the rooms you haven't searched."

"No; she's at a distance." I had made up my mind. "She has gone out."

Mrs. Grose stared.

"Without a hat?"

I naturally looked volumes.

"Isn't that woman always without one?"

"She's with HER?"

"She's with HER!" I declared. "We must find them."

My hand was on my friend's arm, but she failed for the moment, confronted with such an account of the matter, to respond to my pressure. She was rooted, on the spot, with her uneasiness.

"And where's Master Miles?"

"Oh, HE'S with Quint. They're in the school-room."

"Lord, miss!"

My view, I was myself aware—and therefore I suppose my tone—had never yet reached so calm an assurance.

"The trick's been played," I continued; "they've successfully worked their plan. He found the most divine way to keep me quiet while she went off."

"'Divine'?" Mrs. Grose echoed.

"Infernal, then!" I almost cheerfully answered. "He has provided for himself as well. But come!"

She had helplessly looked up at the upper regions.

"You leave him—?"

"So long with Quint? Yes—I don't mind that now."

She always ended, at these moments, by taking hold of my hand, and in this manner she could still stay me.

But, after an instant, shocked at my sudden resignation, she cried, "Because of your letter?"

I quickly, by way of answer, felt for my letter, drew it forth, held it up, and then, freeing myself, went and laid it on the great hall table.

"Luke will take it," I said as I came back.

I reached the house door and opened it; I was already on the steps, but my companion stopped: the storm of the night and early morning had stopped, but the afternoon was damp and gray. I went down to the drive while she stood in the doorway.

"You go with nothing on?"

"What do I care when the child has nothing? I can't wait to dress," I cried, "and if you must do so, I leave you. Try meanwhile, yourself, upstairs."

"With THEM?"

On this, the poor woman promptly joined me!

XIX

We went straight to the lake, as it was called at Bly, though it may in fact have been a sheet of water less remarkable than it appeared. My acquaintance with sheets of water was small, and the pool of Bly, on the few occasions of my consenting, with my pupils, to go out on it in the old flat-bottomed boat moored there, had impressed me both with its area and its occasional waves.

The usual place of leaving to boat on it was half a mile from the house, but I was sure that, wherever Flora might be, she was not near home. She had not given me the slip for any small adventure, and, since the day I had shared with her by the pond, I had been aware, in our walks, of the quarter to which she was most likely to go. This was why I now gave to Mrs. Grose so marked a direction—a direction that made her, when she saw it, oppose it.

"You're going to the water?—you think she's IN—?"

"She may be, though the depth is, I believe, nowhere very great. But what I judge most likely is that she's on the spot from which, the other day, we saw together what I told you."

"When she pretended not to see—?"

"With such self-possession? I'm sure she wanted to go back alone. And now her brother has managed it for her."

Mrs. Grose still stood where she had stopped.

"You suppose they really TALK of them?"

I could meet this with a confidence!

"They say things that, if we heard them, would make us feel sick."

"And if she IS there—"

"Yes?"

"Then Miss Jessel is?"

"Beyond a doubt. You shall see."

"Oh, thank you!" my friend cried, planted so firm that, taking it in, I went straight on without her.

By the time I reached the pool, however, she was close behind me, and I knew that, whatever might happen, my society struck her as her as the least danger. She gave a moan of relief as we at last came in sight of the greater part of the water without a sight of the child.

There was no trace of Flora on the nearer side of the bank where my observation of her had been most startling, and none on the opposite edge where, save for a margin of twenty yards, a thick woods came down to the water. The pond had a width so narrow compared to its length that, with its ends out of view, it might have been taken for a river. We looked at the empty expanse, and then I felt the suggestion of my friend's eyes.

I knew what she meant, and I replied with a negative head-shake, "No, no; wait! She has taken the boat."

My companion stared at the vacant mooring place and then again across the lake.

"Then where is it?"

"Our not seeing it is the strongest of proofs. She has used it to go over, and has managed to hide it."

"All alone—that child?"

"She's not alone, and at such times she's not a child: she's an old, old woman."

I looked at all the shore while Mrs. Grose took again, into the queer element I offered her, one of her plunges of agreement. I pointed out that the boat might perfectly be hidden in a small refuge formed by one of the recesses of the pool, masked on the far side by the bank and by a clump of trees growing close to the water.

"But if the boat's there, where on earth's SHE?" my companion anxiously asked.

"That's exactly what we must learn."

And I started to walk further.

"By going all the way round?"

"Certainly, far as it is. It will take us but ten minutes, but it's far enough to have made the child prefer not to walk. She went straight over."

"Laws!" cried my friend again.

My logic was too much for her, but she dragged at my heels, and when we had got halfway round—a difficult, tiresome process on ground much broken and by a path choked with overgrowth—I paused to give her breath. I helped her with a grateful arm, assuring her that she might hugely help me.

This started us off again, so that in a few minutes more we reached a point from which we found the boat to be where I had supposed. It had been left as much as possible out of sight, and was tied to one of the stakes of a fence that came, just there, down to the brink, and that had been a help in getting on shore.

I recognized, as I looked at the pair of short, thick oars, quite safely drawn up, the difficulty of the feat for a little girl; but I had lived, by this time, too long among wonders to think it impossible. There was a gate in the fence, through which we passed, and that brought us, after a very short time, more into the open.

"There she is!" we both exclaimed at once.

Flora, a short way off, stood before us on the grass, and smiled as if her performance was now complete. The next thing she did, however, was to stoop down and pick—quite as if it were all she was there for—a big, ugly handful of dry grass. But I instantly became sure she had just come out of the woods.

She waited for us, not taking a step, as we slowly approached her. She smiled and smiled, and we met; but it was all done in a silence that, by this time, was very tense. Mrs. Grose was the first to break the spell: she threw herself on her knees and, drawing the child to her, held her tender, yielding body to her breast.

While this dumb show lasted I could only watch—which I did the more intently when I saw Flora's face peep at me over our companion's shoulder. It was serious now—the flicker had left it; but it strengthened the pang with which I at that moment envied Mrs.

Grose the simplicity of HER relation. Nothing more passed between us save that Flora let go of her handful of grass.

What she and I had in effect said to each other was that excuses were useless now. When Mrs. Grose finally got up she kept the child's hand, so that the two were still before me; and the lack of words between us was even more marked in the frank look she gave me.

"I'll be hanged," it said, "if *I*'ll speak!"

It was Flora, gazing at me in wonder, who spoke first. She was struck with our bare-headed look.

"Why, where are your things?"

"Where yours are, my dear!" I quickly returned.

She had already got back her gaiety, and appeared to take this as an answer quite sufficient.

"And where's Miles?" she went on.

There was something in the way she said it that quite finished me: these three words from her were like the glitter of a drawn blade, the trembling of the cup that my hand, for weeks, had held high and full to the brim, that now, even before speaking, I felt over-flow in a burst.

"I'll tell you if you'll tell ME—" I heard myself say, then heard the trembling in which it broke.

"What?"

Mrs. Grose's suspense blazed at me, but it was too late now, and I brought the thing out handsomely.

"Where, my pet, is Miss Jessel?"

XX

JUST AS IN the churchyard with Miles, the whole thing was upon us. Much as I had made of the fact that this name had never once, between us, been spoken, the quick, guilty glare with which the child's face now received it made my breach of the silence like the smash of a pane of glass. It added to the cry, as if to stay the blow, that Mrs. Grose, at the same instant, uttered over my violence. It was the shriek of a creature scared, or wounded, which, in turn, was completed by a cry of my own.

I seized my companion's arm.

She's there, she's there!"

Miss Jessel stood before us on the opposite bank exactly as she had the other time, and I remember, as the first feeling produced in me, my thrill of joy at having brought on proof. She was there, and I was justified; she was there, and I was neither cruel nor mad.

She was there for poor scared Mrs. Grose, but she was there most for Flora; and no moment of my terrible time was perhaps so extraordinary as that in which I threw out to her—with the sense that, pale and hungry demon as she was, she would understand it—a cry of gratitude.

She rose on the spot my friend and I had lately quitted, and there was not, in all the long reach of her desire, an inch of evil that fell short. This first, clear vision were things of a few seconds, during which Mrs. Grose's dazed blink across to where I pointed struck me as a sign that she too at last saw, just as it carried my eyes to the child.

The manner in which Flora was affected startled me, in truth, far more than it would have done to find her also merely stirred, for I had not expected to be disappointed. Prepared and on her guard as our pursuit had actually made her, Flora would avoid every betrayal; and I was therefore shaken by my first glimpse of the particular reaction for which I had not allowed.

To see her, without a sign on her small pink face, not even pretend to glance in the direction of the sight I announced, but, instead, turn at ME an expression of hard, still gravity, an expression absolutely new that appeared to read and accuse and judge me—this was a stroke that somehow changed the little girl herself into the very presence that could make me tremble.

I trembled even though my certainty that she saw was never greater than at that instant, and in the need to defend myself I called her with passion to witness.

"She's there, you little unhappy thing—there, there, THERE, and you see her as well as you see me!"

I had said shortly before to Mrs. Grose that she was not at these times a child, but an old, old woman, and that description of her could not have been more strikingly seen than in the way in which, for answer to this, she simply showed me, without an admission of her eyes, a face of deeper and, indeed, quite fixed, scorn.

I was by this time—if I can put it at all together—more upset at what I may call her manner than anything else, though at the same time I had Mrs. Grose also to deal with. She, the next moment, blotted out everything but her own flushed face and loud, shocked protest.

"What a dreadful turn, to be sure, miss! Where on earth do you see anything?"

I could only grasp her more quickly, for even while she spoke the evil presence stood there clearly, without being frightened away. It had already lasted a minute, and it lasted while I continued, seizing my colleague, thrusting her at it, and presenting her to it with my pointing hand.

"You don't see her exactly as WE see?—you mean to say you don't now—NOW? She's as big as a blazing fire! Only look, dearest woman, LOOK—!"

She looked, even as I did, and gave me, with her deep groan of negation, compassion—the mixture with her pity of her relief at her not seeing what I was pointing at—a sense, touching to me even then, that she would have backed me up if she could. I might well have needed it, for with this blow that her eyes were hopelessly sealed to the proof, I felt my own situation fall apart.

I felt—I saw—the former governess press, from her position, on my defeat, and I knew more of what I should have from this instant to deal with in the refusal to believe attitude of Flora. Into this attitude Mrs. Grose immediately and violently entered, breaking, even while there pierced through my sense of ruin a greater sense of private triumph, a breathless reassurance.

"She isn't there, little lady, and nobody's there—and you never see nothing, my sweet! How can poor Miss Jessel—when poor Miss Jessel's dead and buried? WE know, don't we, love?" she appealed to the child.

"It's all a mistake and a worry and a joke—and we'll go home as fast as we can!" she added.

Flora, on this, responded with a strange, quick sense of what was proper, and with Mrs. Grose she was again on her feet, united, as it were, in opposition to me.

Flora continued to fix me with her small mask of disapproval, and even at that minute I prayed God to forgive me for seeming to see that, as she stood there holding tight to our friend's dress, her childish beauty had suddenly failed, had quite vanished. She was, literally, very ordinary; she had turned common and almost ugly.

"I don't know what you mean. I see nobody. I see nothing. I never HAVE. I think you're cruel. I don't like you!" she cried.

After saying this, which might have been said by a common little girl in the street, she hugged Mrs. Grose closely and buried in her skirts her ugly little face.

In this position she produced an almost angry cry.

"Take me away—take me away from HER!"

"From ME?" I cried.

"From you—from you!" she screamed.

Even Mrs. Grose looked at me, shocked, while I had nothing to do but communicate again with the figure that, on the opposite bank, without a movement, as rigidly still as if catching our voices, was as clearly there for my disaster as it was not there for my service.

The wretched child had spoken exactly as if she had got from some outside source each of her stabbing little words, and I could therefore, in the full despair of all I had to accept, but sadly shake my head at her. If I had ever doubted, all my doubt would at present have gone.

I've been living with the terrible truth, and now it has only too much closed round me.

"Of course I've lost you," I said under my breath. "I've come between you, and you've seen—under HER dictation"— with which I faced, over the pool again, our evil witness—"the easy and perfect way to meet it. I've done my best, but I've lost you. Goodbye."

To Mrs. Grose I said an almost frantic, "Go, go!" before which, in great distress, but silently possessed of the little girl and clearly convinced, in spite of her blindness, that something awful had occurred, she retreated, by the way we had come, as fast as she could.

Of what first happened when I was left alone I have no memory. I only know that at the end of, I suppose, a quarter of an hour, something damp and rough, chilling and piercing, made me realize I must have thrown myself on my face on the ground, and given way to a wild grief.

I must have lay there long, crying and sobbing, for when I raised my head the day was almost done. I got up and looked a moment through the twilight at the gray pool and its blank, haunted edge, and then I took, back to the house, my sad and difficult course.

Flora passed that night, by unspoken arrangement, with Mrs. Grose. I saw neither of them on my return, but, on the other hand, as by way of compensation, I saw a great deal of Miles. I saw—I can use no other phrase—so much of him that it was as if it were more than it had ever been. No evening I had passed at Bly had the importance of this one; in spite of which—and in spite also of the deeper depths of anxiety that had opened beneath me—there was, in the ebbing, a sweet sadness.

On reaching the house I had never so much as looked for the boy; I had simply gone straight to my room to change what I was wearing and to take in, at a glance, much material testimony to Flora's break with me. Her belongings had all been removed.

When later, by the school-room fire, I was served tea by the usual maid, I made no inquiry whatever about my other pupil. Miles had his freedom now—he might have it to the end! Well, he did have it; and it consisted—in part at least—of his coming in at about eight o'clock and sitting down with me in silence.

On the removal of the tea things I had blown out the candles and drawn my chair closer to the fire. I was conscious of a mortal coldness and felt as if I should never again be warm. So, when he appeared, I was sitting in the glow with my thoughts.

He paused a moment by the door as if to look at me; then—as if to share my thoughts—came to the other side of the fire and sank into a chair. We sat there in absolute stillness; yet he wanted, I felt, to be with me.

XXI

BEFORE A NEW day in my room had fully broken, my eyes opened to Mrs. Grose, who had come to my bedside with worse news. Flora was feverish; she had passed a night of extreme unrest, upset above all by fears that had for their subject not her former, but her present, governess.

It was not against the possible return of Miss Jessel on the scene that she protested—it was against me. I was on my feet immediately, of course, and with a great deal to ask, the more that my friend was now prepared to meet me once more. This I felt as soon as I asked about her sense of the child's sincerity as against my own.

"She persists in denying she saw, or has ever seen, anything?"

My visitor's trouble, truly, was great.

"Ah, miss, it isn't a matter on which I can push her! Yet it isn't either, I must say, as if I much needed to. It has made her, every inch of her, quite old."

"Oh, I see her perfectly from here. She resents the question of her truthfulness and, as it were, her respectability. 'Miss Jessel indeed—SHE!' Ah, she's 'respectable,' the chit! The impression she gave me yesterday was, I assure you, the strangest of all; it was quite beyond any of the others. I DID put my foot in it! She'll never speak to me again."

Terrible and dim as it all was, it held Mrs. Grose briefly silent; then she granted my point with a frankness which, I made sure, had more behind it.

"I think miss, she never will. She do have a grand manner about it!"

"And that manner"—I summed it up—"is practically what's the matter with her now!"

Oh, that manner, I could see in my visitor's face!

"She asks me every few minutes if I think you're coming in."

"I see." I, too, on my side, had worked it out. "Has she said since yesterday—except to not knowing anything so dreadful—a single other word about Miss Jessel?"

"Not one, miss. And of course you know," my friend added, "I took it from her, by the lake, that, just then and there at least, there WAS nobody."

"Rather! And, naturally, you take it from her still."

"I don't contradict her. What else can I do?"

"Nothing! You've the cleverest little person to deal with. They've made them—their two friends, I mean—still cleverer even than nature did; for it was wonderful material to play on! Flora has now something to complain about, and she'll work it to the end."

"Yes, miss; but to WHAT end?"

"Why, that of dealing with me to her uncle. She'll make me out to him the lowest creature—!"

I drew back at the fair show on Mrs. Grose's face; she looked for a minute as if she sharply saw them together.

"And him who thinks so well of you!"

"He has an odd way—it comes over me now," I laughed,"—of proving it! But that doesn't matter. What Flora wants, of course, is to get rid of me."

My companion bravely agreed.

"Never again to so much as look at you."

"So what you've come to me now for," I asked, "is to speed me on my way?" Before she had time to reply, however, I had her in check. "I've a better idea—the result of my thinking about it. My going WOULD seem the right thing, and on Sunday I was very near it. Yet that won't do. It's YOU who must go. You must take Flora."

My visitor, at this, did wonder.

"But where in the world—?"

"Away from here. Away from THEM. Away, even most of all, now, from me. Straight to her uncle."

"Only to tell on you—?"

"No, not 'only'! To leave me with my remedy."

She was still not sure what I meant.

"And what IS your remedy?"

"Your loyalty, to begin with. And then Miles's."

She looked at me hard.

"Do you think he—?"

"Won't, if he has the chance, turn on me? Yes, I still think it. At all events, I want to try. Get off with his sister as soon as possible and leave me with him alone."

I was amazed, myself, at the spirit I had still in reserve, and therefore perhaps a trifle the more up-set at the way in which, in spite of this fine example of it, she hesitated.

"There's one thing, of course," I went on. "They mustn't, before she goes, see each other for even three seconds."

Then it came over me that, in spite of Flora's supposed being alone from the instant of her return from the pool, it might already be too late.

"Do you mean," I anxiously asked, "they HAVE met?"

At this she quite flushed.

"Ah, miss, I'm not such a fool as that! If I've had to leave her three or four times, it has been each time with one of the maids, and at present, though she's alone, she's locked in safe. And yet—and yet!"

There were too many things.

"And yet what?"

"Well, are you so sure of the little gentleman?"

"I'm not sure of anything but YOU. But I have, since last evening, a new hope. I think he wants to give me an opening. I do believe that—poor little fellow!—he wants to speak. Last evening, in the firelight and the silence, he sat with me for two hours as if it were just coming."

Mrs. Grose stared through the window at the gray, gathering day.

"And did it come?"

"No, though I waited and waited, it didn't, and it was without a breach of the silence or so much as a faint mention of his sister's condition and absence that we at last kissed good night. All the same," I continued, "I can't, if her uncle sees her, consent to his seeing her brother without my having given the boy—and most of all because things have got so bad—a little more time."

My friend appeared to drag her feet at this more than I could quite understand.

"What do you mean by more time?"

"Well, a day or two—really to bring it out. He'll then be on MY side—of which you see the importance. If nothing comes, I shall only fail, and you will, at the worst, have helped me by doing, on your arrival in town, whatever you may have found possible."

So I put it to her, but she still held back for a little, for no reason that I knew, and I came again to her aid.

"Unless, indeed," I said, "you really want NOT to go."

I could see it in her face, which at last cleared; she put out her hand to me as if to shake on it.

"I'll go—I'll go. I'll go this morning."

I wanted to be very just.

"If you SHOULD wish still to wait, I would make sure she shouldn't see me."

"No, no: it's the place itself. She must leave it." She held me a moment with her eyes, then brought out the rest. "Your idea's the right one. I myself, miss—"

"Well?"

"I can't stay."

The look she gave me made me jump at possibilities.

"You mean that, since yesterday, you HAVE seen—?"

She shook her head with dignity.

"I've HEARD—!"

"Heard?"

"From the child—horrors! There!" she sighed with tragic relief. "On my honor, miss, she says things—!"

With this she broke down; she dropped, with a sudden sob upon my sofa and, as I had seen her do before, gave way to all the grief of it.

It was quite in another manner that I let myself go.

"Oh, thank God!"

She sprang up at this, drying her eyes with a groan.

"'Thank God'?"

"It so justifies me!"

"It does that, miss!"

I couldn't have desired more emphasis, but I hesitated.

"She's so terrible?"

I saw my companion scarce knew how to put it.

"Really shocking."

"And about me?"

"About you, miss—since you must have it. It's beyond everything for a young lady; and I can't think wherever she must have picked up—"

"The terrible language she applied to me? I can!"

I broke in with a laugh that was significant enough. It only, in truth, left my friend still more grave.

"Well, perhaps I ought to also—since I've heard some of it before! Yet I can't bear it," the poor woman went on, while she glanced at my watch on the dressing table.

"But I must go back."

I kept her, however.

"Ah, if you can't bear it—!"

"How can I stop with her, you mean? Why, just FOR that: to get her away. Far from this," she went on, "far from THEM so…"

"She may be different? She may be free?" I seized her almost with joy. "Then, in spite of yesterday, you BELIEVE—"

"In such doings?" Her simple description of them required, in the light of her expression, to be carried no further, and she gave me the whole thing as she had never done. "I believe."

Yes, it was a joy, and we were still shoulder to shoulder: if I might continue sure of that I should care but little what else happened. My support in the presence of disaster would be the same as it had been in my early need of confidence, and if my friend would answer for my honesty, I would answer for all the rest. On the point of her taking leave, nevertheless, I held her back.

"There's one thing, of course—it occurs to me—to remember. My letter, giving the alarm, will have reached town before you."

I now saw still more how she had been beating about the bush and how weary at last it had made her.

"Your letter won't have got there. Your letter never went."

"What then became of it?"

"Goodness knows! Master Miles—"

"Do you mean HE took it?" I gasped.

She hung fire, but she at last overcame it.

"I mean that I saw yesterday, when I came back with Miss Flora, that it wasn't where you had put it. Later in the evening I had the chance to question Luke, and he declared that he had neither noticed nor touched it."

We could only exchange, on this, one of our deeper soundings, and it was Mrs. Grose who first brought it out with an almost elated, "You see!"

"Yes, I see that if Miles took it instead he probably will have read it and destroyed it."

"And don't you see anything else?"

I faced her a moment with a sad smile.

"It strikes me that by this time your eyes are open even wider than mine."

They proved to be so indeed, but she could still blush, almost, to show it.

"I make out now what he must have done at school." And she gave, in her simple sharpness, an almost happy nod. "He stole!"

I turned it over—I tried to be more fair.

"Well—perhaps."

She looked as if she found me unexpectedly calm.

"He stole LETTERS!"

She couldn't know my reasons for a calmness, after all, pretty shallow; so I showed them off as I might.

"I hope then it was to more purpose than in this case! The note, at any rate, that I put on the table yesterday," I went on, "will have given him so little an advantage—for it contained only the bare demand for an interview—that he is already much ashamed of having gone so far for so little, and that what he had on his mind last evening was the need of confession."

I seemed to myself, for the instant, to have mastered it, to see it all. "Leave us, leave us"—I was already, at the door, hurrying her off. "I'll get it out of him. He'll meet me—he'll confess. If he confesses, he's saved. And if he's saved—"

"Then YOU are?"

The woman kissed me on this, and I took her farewell.

"I'll save you without him!" she cried as she went.

XXII

I T WAS WHEN she had got off—and I missed her—that the pinch really came. If I had counted on what it would give me to find myself alone with Miles, I soon saw that it would give me at least a measure of relief. Yet no hour of my stay was so filled with anxiety as that of my coming down to learn that the carriage with Mrs. Grose and my younger pupil had already left.

Now I WAS, I said to myself, face to face with the elements, and for much of the rest of the day, while I fought my weakness, I considered that I might have been foolish. It was a tighter place than I had yet turned round in; all the more that, for the first time, I could see in the faces of others a confused reflection of the crisis.

What had happened naturally caused them all to stare; there was too little explained, say what we might, in the suddenness of my companion's act. The maids and the men looked blank; the effect on my nerves was to worsen them, until I saw the need of making it a positive aid. It was, in short, by clutching the helm that I avoided total wreck; and I dare say that, to bear up at all, I became, that morning, very grand.

I welcomed the idea that I had much to do, and I caused it to be known as well that, left to myself, I was quite firm. I wandered with that manner, for the next hour or two, all over the place, and looked, I have no doubt, as if I were ready for anything that might happen.

The person it appeared least to concern proved to be, till dinner, little Miles himself. My wanderings had given me no glimpse of him, but they tended to make more public the change taking place in our relation as a consequence of his having at the piano, the day before, kept me, in Flora's interest, so charmed.

Everyone knew, of course, of her leaving, and the change itself was now ushered in by our not observing the regular custom of the school-room. Miles himself had already disappeared when, on my way down, I pushed open his door, and I learned below that he had breakfasted—in the presence of a couple of the maids—with Mrs. Grose and his sister.

He had then gone out, as he said, for a walk, which nothing, I reflected, could better have expressed his frank view of the sudden change in my office. What he would not permit this office to consist of was yet to be settled. But there was an odd relief—for myself especially—in giving up one pretension.

If so much had come to the surface, I scarce put it too strongly in saying that what was perhaps most obvious was the foolishness of our continuing with the idea that I had anything more to teach him. He had at any rate his freedom now; I was never to touch it again. Also, I had too much, from this moment, my other ideas.

So the house would know the high state I was in, I declared that my meals with the boy should be served in the dining-room downstairs. Thus it was I found myself waiting for him in the pomp of the room, outside of the window of which I had had from Mrs. Grose that first flash of something that could scarcely be called light.

Here I felt once again how my sense of balance depended on the success of my will, the will to shut my eyes as tight as possible to the truth that what I had to deal with was, in a sick way, against nature. I could only get on at all by treating my ordeal as a push in a direction—unusual, of course, and unpleasant—but demanding, after all, only another turn of the screw.

No attempt could well require more than this to supply, one's self, ALL the nature. How could I put even a little of that into no mention of what had occurred? How, on the other hand, could I mention it without a new plunge into what was both ugly and difficult to talk about? Well, a sort of answer, after a time, came to me, and it was backed up by the fact that I was met, no doubt about it, by a heightened view of what was rare in Miles.

It was indeed as if he had found—as he had so often found at lessons—still some other delicate way to ease me off. Wasn't there light, as we shared our solitude, in the way it broke out in his face with a glitter it had never quite worn before? It would be unbelievable in a child so gifted to not give the help one might get from absolute intelligence. What had his intelligence been given him for but to save him? It was as if, when we were face to face in the dining room, he had shown me the way.

The roast lamb was on the table, and I had asked the servants to leave us. Miles, before he sat down, stood a moment with his hands in his pockets and looked at the roast, on which he seemed about to pass some humorous remark; but what he said instead was, "I say, my dear, is she really very awfully ill?"

"Little Flora? Not so bad but that she'll presently be better. Bly had ceased to agree with her. Come and take your lamb."

He quickly obeyed me, carried the plate carefully to his seat, and, when he was established, went on.

"Did Bly disagree with her so terribly suddenly?"

"Not so suddenly. One had seen it coming on."

"Then why didn't you get her off before?"

"Before what?"

"Before she became too ill to travel."

I found myself quick to answer.

"She's NOT too ill to travel: she might have been if she stayed." This was just the moment to seize. "The journey will take the influence away and carry it off."

"I see, I see," said Miles'

He settled to his meal with the charming little table manners that, from the day of his arrival, had relieved me of all grossness of correcting him. Whatever he had been driven from school for, it was not for ugly feeding. He was perfect, as always, but he was clearly paying more attention to his manners. He was trying to take for granted more things than he found, without help, quite easy; and he dropped into a peaceful silence.

Our meal was brief—and I had the things removed. While this was being done Miles stood again, his back to me, looking out the wide window through which, that other day, I had seen what pulled me up. We continued silent while the maid was with us—as silent, it occurred to me, as a young couple who, on their wedding journey at an inn, feel shy in the presence of the waiter.

He turned round only when the maid had left us.

"Well—so we're alone!"

XXIII

"More or less." I fancy my smile was pale. "Not absolutely. We shouldn't like that!"

"No—I suppose not. Of course, we have the others."

"We have the others," I agreed.

"Yet even though we have them," he returned, still with his hands in his pockets and planted there in front of me, "they don't much count, do they?"

I made the best of it, but I felt washed out.

"It depends on what you call 'much'!"

"Yes," he agreed, "everything depends!"

On this he walked slowly to the window and stayed there a while, with his forehead against the glass, looking out at the dried shrubs and dull trees of November.

By now I had gained the sofa. Steadying myself, I prepared myself for the worst. But an extra-ordinary impression came to me as I gathered a meaning from the boy's back—none other than the impression that I was not barred now. This feeling grew sharper and seemed bound with the idea that it was HE who was. The windows were an image for him of a kind of failure.

I saw him, at any rate, either shut in or shut out. He was admirable, but not comfortable: I took it in with a throb of hope. Wasn't he looking through the window for something he couldn't see?—and wasn't it the first time in the whole business that he had known such a failure?

The first I found a splendid sign. It made him anxious, though he watched himself; he had been anxious all day and, even while in his usual sweet little manner he sat at table, had needed all his genius to give it a shine. When he at last turned round, it was as if he had given in.

"Well, I think I'm glad Bly agrees with ME!"

"You would certainly seem to have seen, these twenty-four hours, a good deal more of it than for some time. I hope," I went on bravely, "you're enjoying yourself."

"Oh, yes, I've been ever so far; all round about—miles and miles. I've never been so free."

He had really a manner of his own, and I could only try to keep up with him.

"Well, do you like it?"

He stood there smiling; then at last he put into two words—"Do YOU?"—more meaning than I had ever heard two words contain. Before I had time to deal with that, however, he continued as if with the sense that this statement should be softened.

"Nothing could be more charming than the way you take it, for of course, if we're alone together now, it's you that are alone most. But I hope," he threw in, "you don't particularly mind!"

"Having to do with you?" I asked. "My dear child, how can I help minding? Though I've given up all claim to your company—you're so beyond me—I at least greatly enjoy it. What else should I stay on for?"

He looked at me more directly, and his face, graver now, struck me as the most beautiful I had ever found it.

"You stay on just for THAT?"

"Certainly. I stay on as your friend, and from the great interest I take in you till something can be done for you that may be more worth your while. That needn't surprise you." My voice trembled so that I felt it impossible to suppress the shake. "Don't you remember how I told you, when I came and sat on your bed the night of the storm, that there was nothing I wouldn't do for you?"

"Yes, yes!" He, on his side, more and more nervous, had a tone to master; but he was so much more successful than I that, laughing through his gravity, he could pretend we were pleasantly jesting. "Only that, I think, was to get me to do something for YOU!"

"It was partly to get you to do something," I agreed. "But, you know, you didn't do it."

"Oh, yes," he said with the brightest eagerness, "you wanted me to tell you something."

"That's it. Straight out. What you have on your mind."

"Ah, then, is THAT what you've stayed over for?"

He spoke with a gaiety through which I could still catch the finest little quiver of bitterness; but I can't begin to express the effect on me of a surrender even so faint. It was as if what I had yearned for had come at last.

"Well, yes—I may as well make a clean breast of it, it was precisely for that."

He waited so long that I supposed it for the purpose of denying me the confidence for which I had stayed; but what he finally said was, "Do you mean now—here?"

"There couldn't be a better place or time."

He looked round him uneasily, and I had the strange impression of the very first sign I had seen in him of the approach of fear. It was as if he were suddenly afraid of me—which struck me as perhaps the best thing to make him. Yet in the effort I felt it foolish to try to be stern, and I heard myself the next instant so gentle as to be almost foolish.

"You want so to go out again?"

"Awfully!"

He smiled at me bravely, and the bravery of it was increased by his actually flushing with pain. He had picked up his hat and stood twirling it in a way that gave me, even as I was just nearly reaching port, an odd sense of the ugliness of what I was doing.

To do it in ANY way was an act of violence, for what did it consist of but laying the idea of guilt on a small helpless creature who had been for me an opening up of the possibilities of beautiful intercourse? Wasn't it base to create for a being so beautiful an ugly reality?

I suppose I now read into our situation a clearness it couldn't have had at the time, for I seem to see our poor eyes already lighted with some spark of the heart-break that was to come. So we circled about, with terrors and a sense of right and wrong, like fighters not daring to close.

But it was for each other we feared! That kept us a little longer suspended and safe.

"I'll tell you everything," Miles said. "I mean I'll tell you anything you like. You'll stay on with me and we'll both be all right, and I WILL tell you—but not now."

"Why not now?"

My insistence turned him from me and kept him once more at his window in silence, during which time, you might have heard a pin drop. Then he was before me again with the air of a person for whom, outside, someone who had to be reckoned with was waiting.

"I have to see Luke."

I had not yet reduced him to quite so vulgar a lie, and I felt ashamed. But, terrible as it was, his lies made up my truth. I managed thoughtfully a few loops of my knitting.

"Well, then, go to Luke, and I'll wait for what you promise. Only, in return for that, satisfy, before you leave me, one very much smaller request."

He looked as if he felt he had succeeded enough to be able still a little to bargain.

"Very much smaller—?"

"Yes, a mere fraction of the whole. Tell me"—oh, I was off-hand, "if, yesterday afternoon, from the table in the hall, you took, you know, my letter."

 XXIV

My sense of how he received this suffered for a minute from something that I can describe only as a split of my attention—a stroke that, as I sprang up, reduced me to the movement of getting hold of him, drawing him close, and, while I fell for support against the nearest piece of furniture, keeping him with his back to the window.

The appearance was full upon us that I had already had to deal with: Peter Quint had come into view like a guard in a prison. The next thing I saw was that, from outside, he had reached the window, and then I knew that, close to the glass and glaring in through it, he offered once more his white face of hell-fire.

It represents but grossly what took place within me at the sight to say that my decision was quickly made; yet I believe that no woman so overwhelmed ever in so short a time recovered her grasp of the ACT. It came to me in the very terror of his presence that the act would be to keep the boy himself from seeing it what I faced and saw.

The inspiration—I can call it by no other name—was that I felt how I MIGHT do that. It was like fighting with a devil for a human soul, and when I had fairly so defined it, I saw how the human soul—held out, in the tremor of my hands, at arm's length—had a perfect dew of sweat on a lovely childish forehead. The face that was close to mine was as white as the face against the glass, and out of it presently came a sound, not low nor weak, but as if from further away, that I drank like a fragrance.

"Yes—I took it."

At this, with a moan of joy, I drew him close; and while I held him I could feel in the sudden fever of his little body the tremendous pulse of his little heart, I kept my eyes on the thing at the window and saw it move. I have likened it to a prison guard, but its slow wheel, for a moment, was rather the movement of a beast held at bay.

My present courage, however, was such that, not too much to let it through, I had to shade, as it were, my flame. Meanwhile the glare of the face was again at the window, fixed as if to watch and wait. It was the confidence that I might now stand up to him, as well as certainty of the child's not knowing, that made me go on.

"What did you take it for?"

"To see what you said about me."

"You opened the letter?"

"I opened it."

My eyes were now, as I held him off, on Miles's own face, in which the collapse of confidence showed me how complete was his uneasiness. What was so great was that at last, by my success, his sense was sealed and his communication with the other stopped: he knew he was in a presence, but knew not of what, and knew still less that I also was, and that I knew.

What did this strain of trouble matter when my eyes went back to the window only to see that it was clear again and—by my personal triumph—the influence defeated? There was nothing there. I felt that the cause was mine and that I should surely get ALL.

"And you found nothing!"—I let my elation out.

He gave a sad, thoughtful little head-shake.

"Nothing."

"Nothing, nothing!" I almost shouted in my joy.

"Nothing, nothing," he sadly repeated.

I kissed his forehead; it was drenched.

"So what have you done with it?"

"I burned it."

"Burned it?" It was now or never. "Is that what you did at school?"

Oh, what this brought up!

"At school?"

"Did you take letters?—or other things?"

"Other things?" He appeared now to be thinking of something far off that reached him only through the pressure of his anxiety. Yet it did reach him.

"You mean did I STEAL?"

I felt myself redden to the roots of my hair as well as wonder if it were stranger to put to a gentleman such a question, or to see him take it with allowances that gave the very distance of his fall in the world.

"Was it for that you mightn't go back?"

The only thing he felt was a dreary little surprise.

"Did you know I mightn't go back?"

"I know everything."

He gave me at this the longest and strangest look.

"Everything?"

"Everything. Therefore DID you—?"

But I couldn't say it again.

Miles could, very simply.

"No. I didn't steal."

My face must have shown I believed him; yet my hands—but it was for pure tenderness—shook him as if to ask him why, if it was all for nothing, he had made me suffer months of torment.

"What then did you do?"

He looked in vague pain round the top of the room and drew his breath, two or three times, as if with difficulty. He might have been standing at the bottom of the sea and raising his eyes to some faint green twilight.

"Well—I said things."

"Only that?"

"They thought it was enough!"

"To turn you out for?"

Never, truly, had a person "turned out" shown so little to explain it as this little person! He appeared to weigh my question, but in a manner quite detached and helpless.

"Well, I suppose I oughtn't."

"But to whom did you say them?"

He tried to remember, but it dropped—he had lost it.

"I don't know!"

He almost smiled at me in the unhappiness of his surrender, which was indeed practically, by this time, so complete that I ought to have left it there. But I was blind with victory, though even then the very effect that was to have brought him so much nearer was already that of added separation.

"Was it to everyone?" I asked.

"No; it was only to—" But he gave a sick little head-shake. "I don't remember their names."

"Were they then so many?"

"No—only a few. Those I liked."

Those he liked? I seemed to float not into clearness, but into something darker, and within a minute there came to me out of my pity the alarm of his being perhaps innocent. It was for an instant puzzling and without a bottom, for if he WERE innocent, what then on earth was *I*? Frozen, while it lasted, by the mere brush of the question, I let him go a little, so that, with a deep-drawn sigh, he turned away from me again.

As he faced toward the clear window, I suffered, feeling that I had nothing now there to keep him from.

"And did they repeat what you said?" I went on.

He was soon at some distance from me, still breathing hard, and again with the air, though now without anger, of being held against his will. Once more, as he had done before, he looked up at the dim day as if, of what had before sustained him, nothing was left but an unspeakable anxiety.

"Oh, yes," he replied—"they must have repeated them. To those THEY liked," he added.

There was, somehow, less of it than I had expected.

"And these things came round—?"

"To the masters? Oh, yes!" he answered very simply. "But I didn't know they'd tell."

"The masters? They didn't—they've never told. That's why I ask you."

He turned to me again his little beautiful fevered face.

"Yes, it was too bad."

"Too bad?"

"What I suppose I sometimes said. To write home."

I can't name the sadness this gave to such a speech by such a speaker; I only know that the next instant I heard myself throw off with homely force, "Stuff and nonsense!"

But what I said after that must have sounded stern enough.

"What WERE these things?"

My sternness was all for his judge, his executioner; yet it made him turn away again, and that movement made ME, with a single bound and cry, spring upon him. For there again, against the glass, as if to spoil his confession and stay his answer, was the hideous author of our woe—the white face of hell-fire.

I felt sick at the drop of my victory and the return of my battle, so that the wildness of my leap only served as a great betrayal. I saw Miles, from the midst of my act, meet it with a sense of what it meant, but that even now he only guessed, and that the window was still to his own eyes free. I let the impulse flame up to convert the climax of his dismay into the very proof of his liberation.

"No more, no more, no more!" I shrieked to the image as I tried to press Miles against me.

"Is she HERE?"

Miles panted as he caught with his sealed eyes the direction of my words. Then as his strange "she" staggered me, with a gasp, I echoed it, "Miss Jessel, Miss Jessel!" He with a sudden fury gave me it back.

I seized, shocked, his guess—some sequel to what we had done to Flora, but this made me only want to show him that it was better still than that.

"It's not Miss Jessel! But it's at the window—straight before us. It's THERE—the terror, for the last time!"

At this, after a second in which his head made the movement of a baffled dog's on a scent and then gave a frantic little shake for air and light, he was at me in a white rage, bewildered, glaring over the place and missing it wholly, though it now, to my sense, filled the room like a taste of poison, the overwhelming presence.

"It's HE!"

"Whom do you mean by 'he'?"

"Peter Quint—you devil!" I cried.

His face gave, round the room, its convulsed look.

"WHERE?"

They are in my ears still, his supreme surrender of the name and his tribute to my devotion.

"What does he matter now, my own?—what will he EVER matter? *I* have you," I launched at the beast, "but he has lost you forever!" Then, for the demonstration of my work, "There, THERE!" I said to Miles.

But he had already jerked straight round, stared again, and seen but the quiet day. With the stroke of the loss I was so proud of, he uttered the cry of a creature hurled over an abyss, and the grasp with which I recovered him might have been that of catching him in his fall.

I caught him, yes, I held him—it may be imagined with what a passion; but at the end of a minute I began to feel what it truly was that I held. We were alone with the quiet day, and his little heart, dispossessed, had stopped.

Printed in the United States
By Bookmasters